Winnie swallowed hard. "How can I know if you…if you really…you know, feel that way?"

"Feel what way?" Grant asked.

"You know what way," she replied quietly. "Attraction and desire. I don't want to be with someone who has to fake it."

Grant stepped forward and touched her shoulder. A simple gesture. One he'd done countless times. Meant to reassure and comfort. But this time…

"There's nothing fake about this, Winnie."

"You can s⸺ ⸺⸺ ⸺⸺ ⸺ ⸺⸺rant, but it doe⸺ ⸺⸺ ⸺⸺ ⸺⸺ change *us*. It d⸺ ⸺⸺ ⸺⸺ ⸺⸺ that you've neve⸺ ⸺⸺ ⸺⸺ ⸺r than your best⸺

He to⸺ ⸺⸺ ⸺⸺y with the back of his hand, desperate suddenly to curve his hand over the safe place where their baby was growing. To feel their child. To feel Winnie.

"I'm pretty sure this disputes that idea," he said. "You want proof?" he asked and took her hand, resting her palm against his chest. "That's my heart, beating like crazy because I'm this close to you. Because I do want you…very much."

* * *

THE CULHANES OF CEDAR RIVER:
Family lost, family found

Dear Reader,

Welcome back to Cedar River, South Dakota! And to my latest book for Harlequin Special Edition, *The Night That Changed Everything*. This is the fifth book in my new series, The Culhanes of Cedar River, and I'm so delighted to have the opportunity to share Grant and Winona's story with you.

I've always loved friends-to-lovers stories—who can ever get enough *When Harry Met Sally*, right? I think there's something magical about watching two people who think they know everything about each other discover there's a whole lot more to their relationship. Which is exactly what happens between Grant Culhane and his best friend, Winona Sheehan. Everything seems to be going exactly as it should be—he's clearly afraid of commitment and she's planning on marrying someone else!

But when love and friendship are so intertwined, nothing is that simple. There's a Vegas wedding, an AWOL fiancé and, a little while later, the repercussions of one wild and very unexpected night. Just friends? Not anymore. As they navigate through the changes in their relationship, they learn a lot about the friendship they've always cherished and the love that clearly defines them both.

I hope you enjoy Grant and Winona's story, and I invite you back to South Dakota for my next book in The Culhanes of Cedar River series, coming soon. I love hearing from readers and can be contacted at helenlaceyauthor@gmail.com or via my website, helenlacey.com, or my Facebook page to talk about horses, cowboys or how wonderful it is writing for Harlequin Special Edition. Happy reading!

Warmest wishes,

Helen Lacey

The Night That Changed Everything

HELEN LACEY

Recycling programs
for this product may
not exist in your area.

ISBN-13: 978-1-335-40795-5

The Night That Changed Everything

Copyright © 2021 by Helen Lacey

All rights reserved. No part of this book may be used or reproduced in
any manner whatsoever without written permission except in the case of
brief quotations embodied in critical articles and reviews.

This is a work of fiction. Names, characters, places and incidents
are either the product of the author's imagination or are used fictitiously.
Any resemblance to actual persons, living or dead, businesses,
companies, events or locales is entirely coincidental.

This edition published by arrangement with Harlequin Books S.A.

For questions and comments about the quality of this book,
please contact us at CustomerService@Harlequin.com.

Harlequin Enterprises ULC
22 Adelaide St. West, 40th Floor
Toronto, Ontario M5H 4E3, Canada
www.Harlequin.com

Printed in U.S.A.

Helen Lacey grew up reading *Black Beauty* and *Little House on the Prairie*. These childhood classics inspired her to write her first book when she was seven, a story about a girl and her horse. She loves writing for Harlequin Special Edition, where she can create strong heroes with soft hearts and heroines with gumption who get their happily-ever-afters. For more about Helen, visit her website, helenlacey.com.

Books by Helen Lacey

Harlequin Special Edition

The Culhanes of Cedar River

The Secret Between Them
The Nanny's Family Wish
The Soldier's Secret Son
When You Least Expect It

The Cedar River Cowboys

Three Reasons to Wed
Lucy & the Lieutenant
The Cowgirl's Forever Family
Married to the Mom-to-Be
The Rancher's Unexpected Family
A Kiss, a Dance & a Diamond
The Secret Son's Homecoming

The Fortunes of Texas: The Hotel Fortune

Their Second-Time Valentine

The Fortunes of Texas: The Lost Fortunes

Her Secret Texas Valentine

Visit the Author Profile page
at Harlequin.com for more titles.

For Robert

Soul Mate...Best Mate

I love that we share this life together.

Chapter One

"I'm getting married!"

Grant Culhane pulled his cell phone away from his ear for a second in disbelief.

Winona. Getting married? Since when?

They spoke most nights, around dinnertime, and had done so for years. Growing up, Winona Sheehan was the best friend he'd ever had—and that hadn't changed much as they'd gotten older.

He digested what she'd said, got a twitch in his gut he didn't waste time registering and then scowled again. "Who the hell to?"

Grant heard her soft sigh. "To Dwight, of course."

The boyfriend. More accurately, the long-distance boyfriend, a marine who was currently deployed in

Bahrain. "Winnie, you haven't seen him in nearly a year. Don't you think you should spend some time together before you start planning a wedding?"

"I'm not *planning* anything," she said. "We're eloping."

Grant's back immediately straightened. "What?"

"I'm heading to Nevada tomorrow and meeting Dwight in Vegas on Thursday. He's got a few days' leave."

She sounded happy. Happier than he'd heard her in a long time, actually. But still, marrying someone who had been in another country for over *ten* of the eighteen months you'd been dating didn't seem like such a great idea.

"Winnie," he said, dropping his voice an octave and using the nickname, funnily, that only *he* called her. "Don't you think you should—"

"I'm tired of thinking," she said, clearly exasperated as she cut off his words. "I overthink *everything*. That's why I work in a boring job and have never ventured past the South Dakota state line. I'm sick of playing it safe. Dwight asked me to marry him and I said yes, so you could at least pretend to be happy for me."

"Of course I'm happy for you," he lied, since he wasn't feeling that way inclined at all. Damn if he couldn't figure out why.

"Are you gonna be there or not?" she asked abruptly, cutting him off again. "Dwight's bringing his best friend from his unit, and to be honest, I'd like my best friend to be there, too. Can you get the time off work?"

Grant pushed back in his chair. He looked around at the four bland office walls. He'd been working fourteen-hour days on the same job for over a week and suspected he could certainly use a break. Plus, there was the current family drama that was taking up way too much of his thinking time lately.

Still, he wasn't sure how he felt about seeing Winnie get married, either!

But how could he say no to her?

"Of course I can be there by Thursday," he said, surprising himself a little.

He heard her relieved sigh and then felt better about his decision. If he was there, at least he had a shot at trying to talk her out of it, or maybe he could have a word with Dwight and get the other man to see that eloping wasn't a great idea. For starters, Winona's grandfather would certainly have something to say about his only grandchild racing off to marry a man she had only seen in the flesh a handful of times.

"Have you told Red?" he asked.

She sighed. "No. You know how he is. He's going to ask me to wait so we can have a proper wedding."

"He'd have a point."

"It *will* be a proper wedding," she replied. "All that matters is that Dwight and I want to do this now. Besides, he's only got four days leave and Papa wouldn't be able to travel that far on such short notice."

That was true. Red Sheehan's health wasn't the best. The older man had been the foreman on Grant's family's ranch for years before a series of strokes forced him to stop working altogether. He still lived on the ranch, though, and helped out where he could. Grant's oldest brother, Mitch, would always offer a home for the Sheehans on the Triple C.

"I'll call you tonight," Winona said and ended the call.

Grant slipped the phone into his pocket, got to his feet and walked to the window, staring out to the street below. He stretched out his shoulders, thinking about Winnie, his concern quickly gathering momentum. Of course, after nearly twenty years of friendship, he'd never known her to be impulsive—Grant didn't even know if she really loved the guy. Sure, she regularly talked about the marine, but he wasn't convinced she was doing the right thing by marrying him.

He wondered whether he should have tried to talk her out of it, or at least tried harder to get her to hold off for a few more months. The truth was, he probably should have seen it coming. But he'd been distracted lately—with work, with family stuff—and maybe he'd been too preoccupied to focus on what was going on in his best friend's relationship. He'd try and get to the bottom of things once he saw her, he told himself—even if that was going to be on her wedding day.

He pushed back at the niggling jolt racing up and

down his spine and worked out his next move—go to Vegas and try and talk some sense into her.

After that, maybe he'd go home for a while. He'd lived in Rapid City for seven years, moving there after completing four years of college in Sioux Falls. But Cedar River, South Dakota, would always be home. Situated in the shadow of the Black Hills, it had once been a vibrant mining town. Now, it was mostly a stopover for tourists and commuters heading for the state line. There were several tourist attractions, though, including the famous O'Sullivan Hotel, numerous dude ranches and a couple of the old mines, now operating as tourist centers. Grant loved Cedar River and, more importantly, he loved the Triple C Ranch and his family. The second youngest of six children, he looked up to his older brothers, particularly Mitch, who had gained guardianship of them all when their father had bailed. Grant had been just twelve years old at the time, and still remembered the day his father left. He'd raced after his father's truck, begging him to take him with him. It was a memory Grant tucked away, determined to keep buried.

If only Billie-Jack would let him.

Billie-Jack Culhane had been a deadbeat dad twenty years ago and Grant had no reason to think he'd changed. Except that two weeks earlier, out of the blue, he'd received a call from his long-lost father.

He hadn't recognized the number and let it go to voice mail. The message was short and to the point— Billie-Jack wanted to reconnect. Numb, he hadn't a clue how to react to the memories that he'd struggled for years to hide and which had quickly resurfaced. Three days later, Billie-Jack called again. But Grant wasn't going to be pushed into seeing him. And he knew any of his four older brothers and younger sister, Ellie, wouldn't be interested in seeing the old man, either. No, it was better he kept the information to himself for a while. Besides, now that Winona had dropped her bombshell he had other things to think about.

Grant sighed, stretched out his shoulders again and walked back around the desk. It was going to be a long afternoon, he figured, and sat down. He usually had no trouble concentrating on his work. He liked his job and the company he'd been employed with for the last few years. He'd loved gaming as a kid, but in high school, one of his science teachers noted his skills and encouraged him to pursue computer science as a career. Intrigued, he took the teacher's advice. Now, he worked wherever the company sent him, doing program design and sometimes high-end tech support and program installation for companies up and down the west coast. He had an apartment in Rapid City and spent most of his time there, traveling when needed. And he liked his life. He had a nice home. Good friends. Money in the bank. Yeah, life was sweet.

Except…his father wanted to make a comeback.

And Winnie was getting married. To some guy she hardly knew, no less.

Well, he'd just have to talk to her again—to make sure she was certain that marrying the marine was what she really wanted.

With his mind set on a plan, Grant got back to work and managed to push through until the end of the day.

He was home by six, showered and eating a swiftly put together stir-fry by seven-thirty. Nothing he did, though, could push thoughts of Winnie from his mind.

He wasn't sure why, but the idea of her getting married made his insides churn. It was just his protective instincts jumping into action, that's all, he figured. Of course he wanted to make sure she was safe. He cared about her. After all, they'd grown up together on the Triple C. They were best friends. They knew everything about each other. And he certainly would never have expected this kind of bombshell from her. Most days he forgot she actually had a boyfriend, since the marine was half a world away and she hadn't seen him too often during the months they'd dated.

He and Winnie had been there for each other for as long as Grant could remember, for everything. She taught him how to throw a curveball in middle school; he'd taught her how to ace a math quiz. He'd been the shoulder she'd cried on when she was dumped by her first boyfriend. She'd been the first person he'd called when he'd discovered he was valedictorian in senior year. He teased her when she got braces; she dissed his taste in music.

They talked about everything, from bad dates, religion, the environment, to her insistence that one of his work colleagues had a thing for him. The plus one for weddings and parties. That one friend who mattered above all others. They'd supported one another through loss, grief, heartbreak and failed romances. Yeah…they were best friends, and even if he didn't agree with her planned elopement, he'd still be there for her. Because no matter what, she would do the same for him.

Not that Grant had any plans to get married… *ever*.

After dinner, he booked a flight to Vegas and then picked up his cell and called her. She didn't answer and he didn't bother leaving a message. He was just starting to type out a text message when she called him back.

"Hey, there," she said. "Sorry I missed your call. I was in the middle of sending Dwight a message."

Grant bit back a comment. "No problem. Okay, I'll be at the hotel around three o'clock," he told her. "I'll text you when I'm there."

"Okay, great," she said and then hesitated, her voice scratchy.

"What's wrong?" he asked.

"I feel bad for not telling Papa. And Ellie," she added. "You know how she loves organizing things like this."

That was true. Grant's little sister was a party-planner extraordinaire. "They'll get over it," he assured her, ignoring the sudden and ever-present twitch in his gut. "Once they see how happy the marine makes you."

She laughed. "You know, he does have a name."

"I know," Grant said humorlessly. "I'm just giving you a hard time about it. I hope he appreciates you, Winnie."

"He loves me," she replied and sighed. "That's all I want."

Grant figured that's all anyone wanted. But he'd never been a great believer in the idea of true love. Sure, he believed in attraction and lust and he liked sex as much as the next person, but love always seemed to fade. And worse, ruin lives. He'd watched his father fall to pieces when his mother had died. He'd witnessed his brother Mitch endure divorce from the only woman he'd ever loved. Even though Mitch and Tess were back together now, that didn't erase the years of pain in between. And when his other brother Joss had lost his young wife to cancer, he'd been put through hell by his in-laws as they tried to gain custody of Joss's two daughters. Yeah... love wasn't for him.

"Winnie," he said after a moment. "Are you sure you're—"

"Positive," she replied, cutting him off. "And promise me you're not just coming tomorrow to try and talk me out of it?"

Grant held off for a second, figuring she'd know exactly what he planned on doing. "Well, I only—"

"I know what I'm doing," she assured him. "Please support me in this."

Grant's gut plummeted. Despite his misgivings, he knew he would absolutely support Winnie if she wanted to tie herself to the marine. It was her life. Her choice. And as her friend, he'd support that—even if the idea tied his stomach into knots.

"Okay," he relented. "I promise."

He heard her relieved sigh. "Don't tell Krystal you're heading to Vegas, though," she teased, "or she'll be booking herself on the flight with you."

Krystal Heller worked for the same company he did and although she was nice enough, pretty and friendly, and had made it clear she was interested in him, he wasn't feeling anything other than a respectful working relationship. And he'd never believed in messing around with someone he worked with—it had complication written all over it.

"Give it a rest, will you."

She chuckled. "I'll see you tomorrow," she said and chatted on excitedly for another few seconds before signing off. "Love ya," she said, the same words she ended the call with every night.

"Ditto," Grant replied, as he always did, and then realized something that was oddly unsettling—that it might be the last time he said it to her. She would be married—another man's wife. She'd move to a new town. Probably a new state. And he would rarely see her. Their nightly phone calls would cease. She wouldn't be the last voice he heard before he fell asleep each night.

And he couldn't figure out why the mere idea of that cut through him so hard that for a moment he could barely breathe.

Life was about doing what made a person happy, Winona Anabel Sheehan thought as she looked around the Las Vegas hotel room.

And taking chances.

Not that she'd taken a lot of risks over the years, but that was about to change. She had a lot to be thankful for. First and foremost, she loved three things. Her grandfather, Cedar River and Grant Culhane. Well, of course she actually loved all the Culhanes—but Grant was extra-special to her. He was her best friend.

Four things she loved, she corrected, shaking her head as she carefully draped her wedding gown across the bed. She loved Dwight Kelly, too. He was good-looking and funny and she'd fallen head over heels for him eighteen months ago. He'd been in Cedar River visiting a friend and they'd met at Rusty's bar, hitting it off immediately. Originally from New Mexico, he'd joined the marines at nineteen. He was finishing his current tour in three months, but insisted he didn't want to wait that long to get married. Winona had accepted his proposal via Skype without a second thought. When he finished his tour they would settle at Fort Liggett, California, for a while and Winona was looking forward to the move. She'd lived in Cedar River all of her life, only venturing as far as Sioux Falls for a couple of years to attend a community college there. Yeah, she was about as *hometown* as a girl could get, and at twenty-six was more than ready to venture out into the world.

Papa will understand, she said to herself. Red Sheehan had raised her since her mother ran out when she was nine. Winona didn't know her father, only that he was Brazilian and her mom had hooked up with him in Reno for a weekend and she was the result of that tryst. She knew his first name, which was Paolo. But no surname. No picture. She'd accepted his absence from her life long ago—just like she'd accepted having a mother who didn't really want her. But she had Red, the greatest grandparent in the world. And she had the Culhanes, too. Particularly Grant, and Ellie, who was more like a sister than a friend.

And now she had Dwight—her future husband.

Winona stared at the satin-and-lace gown the saleswoman had said flattered her figure, and pushed down the hankering she had for something more traditional. It didn't matter what she wore. All that mattered was that she would be standing at an altar with the man she loved.

With both of them!

Oh, God, snap out of it, girl!

Winona shook off the thought. As a teenager she'd

secretly and longingly pined for Grant Culhane to look at her as something other than his best friend—only admitting the truth in the diary she wrote in—but never letting Grant know how she felt. As she grew up, she accepted that she was in the friend zone and that's where she would stay. She stood by and watched him fall in love with a girl in high school, and then fall out of love just as swiftly. She remained his sidekick as he hooked up with one woman or another over the last decade, always ending the relationship within a couple of months. Grant didn't do serious. He didn't do commitment and he certainly would *never* do marriage. But he was the shoulder she always cried on. And she did love him—but she wasn't *in love* with him anymore, like she had been back in high school. That would be an obvious waste of her time. Now she was in love with Dwight. It had worked out exactly as it should have.

Her cell pinged and she grabbed the phone, recognizing Grant's number.

I'm in the foyer and all checked in.

Winona's heart skipped a beat. The hotel wasn't the flashiest in Vegas—but it was the best she could afford. She'd told Dwight she would make all of the arrangements, including booking the honeymoon suite. The room was huge and almost hideously decorated in shades of lime green, gold and red, with embossed velvet curtains and ornate furnishings. She was sure Grant would have something to say about the outrageous color scheme—not that she expected him to see the suite. No, she'd be sharing the room with her husband in just over five hours. Dwight was on his way. He'd called her that morning and they spoke briefly, making arrangements to meet at the chapel. Winona had thrilled at hearing his voice, and suggested they catch up at the hotel first, but he'd teased her, saying it was bad luck to see one another on their wedding day.

She grabbed her key card and tote and quickly left the room, heading downstairs to the foyer. The place was busy, and she noticed a bride and groom walking toward the elevators. Newlyweds were certainly in plentiful supply in Vegas. Winona spotted Grant immediately—he was hard to miss! Well over six feet, dark hair, broad shoulders and dark green eyes that were blisteringly intense. She saw a few women glancing at him appreciatively. He was hot, no doubt about that.

He hauled her into a hug the moment they collided and held her close. His arms had always made her feel safe and she hung on tightly for a few extra seconds. He smelled good, too, his cologne woodsy and familiar.

"What?" he said when he released her, holding her a little away, and looking at her jeans and shirt. "No bridal gown?"

"It's upstairs," she replied and laughed. "Don't want to get it wrinkled before the big event."

He glanced at his watch. "Countdown in two hours. Enough time for us to have a drink and catch up."

She gripped his arm. "As long as you keep your promise not to try and talk me out of it?"

He sighed. "I'll do my best. Where's the marine?" he asked and looked around.

"Dwight will be here soon," she assured him, thinking that he never used the other man's name. "He's meeting me at the chapel. He said it was more romantic that way."

Grant rolled his eyes a little. "Okay, Winnie, let's find a cozy spot at the bar over there and you can tell me exactly why you want to marry this guy."

"You know why," she refuted and walked him toward one of the bistros. "He loves me. I love him. That's why people usually get married."

The hotel was busy and several people were milling outside the bistro, but Grant quickly wrangled them a booth seat inside. He ordered drinks—an imported beer for himself and wine spritzer for Winona, her usual when they went out.

"Did you tell anyone?" she asked once the waitress left their booth.

Grant tapped several fingertips on the table. "You asked me not to breathe a word of your plans, remember?"

One thing she knew for certain—she could trust Grant. "Thank you."

"So, what happens after the wedding?" he asked. "Are you coming back to Cedar River?"

"In a few days," Winona said and nodded. "Dwight has to head back on Monday, so I'll return home then and probably stay for a couple of months. His tour finishes in seven weeks. After that I'll move with him to Fort Liggett."

"California?" He raised both brows. "That's a long way from South Dakota."

"It's only for a couple of years. After that, we'll probably come back to Cedar River and settle down. Dwight plans on leaving the army and, once we have kids, I want to make sure we're close to Papa. I think I told you that Dwight's parents are divorced, and since he hardly sees his dad and his mom got remarried, he's happy to live in Cedar River."

Grant leaned back in the seat, one hand around the untouched beer. "Sounds like you've got it all figured out."

She didn't miss the judgment in his tone and shrugged. "I've got plans for the future, like *most* people."

His mouth flattened. "If that's a dig, I'm not biting."

"I guess some people just aren't the marrying kind," she said and sighed. "But I am."

"Which is why you've agreed to marry a guy you haven't seen for the last ten months," he said quietly.

Winona frowned. "I know what I'm doing.

Dwight is a good man. Once you get to really know him, you'll think so, too."

He didn't look convinced and it was exactly what she expected. Grant was concerned about her and she understood why he had reservations. To an outsider, it might look as though she didn't know Dwight all that well. True, they hadn't spent a lot of physical time together since they first met, but he'd visited her in Cedar River a couple of times in the first six months of their relationship. And they talked every week, and texted almost every day, while he was deployed.

"We'll see," Grant said and sipped his beer and then sighed heavily. "Okay...I'll try."

"And you'll behave yourself when we're at the chapel, won't you?" she urged, feeling a little panic rise up and curdle in her belly. Since she'd been surprisingly calm since Dwight had proposed, the sudden attack of nerves startled her. She didn't want to have doubts. She didn't want to live a life with her glass half-empty. She wanted stability, family, real love. And she wasn't going to let her commitment-phobic best friend make her feel any different. "I mean, you are kind of my maid of honor, after all."

He looked appalled by the idea. "If that's what you wanted, you should have invited Ellie along to this gig."

Winona loved Ellie like a sister, but the other woman had a reputation for speaking her mind. "Ellie would have blabbed to your family and to my grandfather. You know you're the only one I trust."

Her words made him stare directly at her. "I just don't want to see you get hurt."

"I won't," she assured him. "But I appreciate that you're looking out for me."

"I always will."

She knew that. "You know, Dwight knows how important you are to me."

That much was true. Although her fiancé wasn't entirely thrilled about her close friendship with Grant. For a while she suspected Dwight wasn't convinced that their relationship was strictly platonic. But it was. It always had been.

"Where's your engagement ring?" he asked, looking at her bare left hand.

Winona shrugged. "There wasn't time for that. And the chapel said they could supply wedding bands."

He raised a quizzical brow. "Did you purchase the complete bridal package online?"

She smiled. "Something like that."

"Organized down to the last detail, I see," he said and grinned.

She smiled. "You know me."

He nodded. "That I do. You know, I'm gonna miss you when you leave for California."

Winona met his gaze and her throat tightened. She'd been so caught up in the excitement of Dwight's online proposal, she hadn't taken much time to think about the consequences. Like living in another state, or being away from her grandfather for the first time in years, or being separated from the only home she'd ever known. From her grandfather. From her friends. Especially Grant.

"I'll miss you, too," she said, feeling the meaning of her words down to the soles of her feet. "More than I can bear thinking about. We've been a part of each other's lives since we were kids."

"Since Red took in his wildcat granddaughter," Grant reminded her. "You were what…eight years old?"

"Nine," she corrected. "And you were twelve. Do you remember finding me in the hayloft that first day?"

He nodded. "Yeah…you were angry at the world."

"But you understood," Winona said as the memory kicked in, tightening her throat. "Because you'd been there yourself. And you're right, I was angry and hurt. My mom had just left me. But you were kind to me that day. You talked me down from the loft and taught me how to halter a horse."

Winona recalled the moment as if it were yesterday. Her mother had dropped her at the ranch, with nothing but a pink backpack and her favorite books. It was just for a few weeks, she'd said. Looking back, Winona knew her grandfather didn't believe it. And when her mom finally made contact over twelve months later, Winona chose to stay with her grandfather after that. Looking back, it was the right decision—even though at the time she'd experienced the range of emotions associated with being abandoned by her only parent. And still did, she suspected. But rationally, she knew she'd had a much happier childhood growing up at the Triple C with Red than she would have had she stayed with her mother. The first day had been hard—but Grant had made her feel so welcome, so much a part of things—and from that first day she developed a little bit of hero worship.

Over time, that turned into a serious crush—and by her thirteenth birthday she was convinced he was the love of her life.

Silly, she supposed, to think about that now, just as she was about to marry Dwight.

Thinking about her fiancé made her sit up straight and then shuffle out of the booth. "I have to get ready," she said. "Meet me in the foyer in an hour."

"How are we getting to the chapel?"

She checked her watch. "Taxi."

Winona took off and headed back to her room. Once she was inside, she showered, slipped into the white lace underwear she'd splurged on, before doing her hair and makeup. Not too much, since most days she went makeup free, but she swept her long black hair into an updo and added the pearl earrings Grant had given her for her eighteenth birthday. She stepped into her lace gown, which was long and figure hugging, off the shoulder in design, and pushed her breasts up in a flattering way.

Giving herself one final look, she double-checked her purse to make sure she had all the documentation she needed and then headed downstairs. Since brides in white gowns were obviously the norm for the hotel, she barely got a glance from the people she passed in the corridor, or in the elevator. Although one older lady did smile and say she looked lovely.

Grant was waiting for her in the foyer and gave her a long and appreciative look.

"You look beautiful," he said when she reached him.

Winona took in his dark suit, white shirt and tie and raised a brow. "You look pretty good yourself."

He smiled. "Do you have everything?"

She nodded and rattled her purse. "Just need to get to my groom."

"Lead the way," he said and grasped her elbow.

Ten minutes later they were at the Love Is All Around Wedding Chapel. There was a couple just finishing their ceremony and Winona watched from the waiting area, nerves settling big-time in her belly. She looked around, noticing how quaint and nicely decorated the place was, and thought it looked exactly like it had online.

The couple at the altar came out arm in arm, laughing happily, and nodded in their direction, with the minister and a well-dressed middle-aged woman following in their wake, throwing confetti. Once the other couple were out of the chapel, the minister approached her and she confirmed their appointment.

And waited for her future husband.

At ten minutes to four, when Dwight still hadn't turned up, Winona got twitchy. "I'm sure I told him

3:45," she said to Grant and looked at the time on her cell again. "The minister said we needed about fifteen minutes to fill out the paperwork."

"He's only five minutes behind schedule. Maybe his flight was held up, or he's at the hotel changing into a suit."

She shook her head and called Dwight's number. "He's wearing his dress uniform. But you're right, he's probably caught up in traffic or something."

When the call went to his voice mail, she left a message and then sat back down, the uneasiness in her stomach increasing as the minutes ticked by. And then, after she tried his cell twice more and the time clicked past four o'clock, Winona knew something wasn't right.

The minister approached her at ten minutes past four and said he had another ceremony booked in twenty minutes and couldn't hold the spot much longer. Winona was about to call his number again when her cell pinged with a text message. She looked at the caller ID. It was from Dwight. Her stomach churned and then she took a breath. She was imagining the worst for no reason. He was late, that's all. He was stuck in traffic or his flight was delayed. Right?

Except, when she read his message, her hopes were crushed.

I'm so sorry, Win. I just can't do it. I'm not ready for a commitment like this. I know you probably hate me right now, but this is for the best. I'm sorry. D.

Her hand shook and she gasped, pressing her other hand to her chest.

"Winnie?"

Grant's voice. Suddenly, he was sitting beside her and she turned to face him, her hand still shaking. She held the phone up and shuddered out a reply. "He...he's not coming."

"What the hell are you talking about?" he asked in disbelief.

She shoved the phone at him with a shaking hand. "Read it."

He took a couple of seconds and then wrapped his hand around hers, placing the phone in her lap. "Winnie, I'm so sorry. But...maybe this *is* for the best."

"I don't understand...he promised..."

Winona's insides hurt so much she could barely breathe. And then, somehow, Grant's arm came around her and she dropped her head to his shoulder. He held her, murmuring that he'd take care of everything, he'd make sure she wouldn't be alone. Oddly, despite the hurt and the chaos screeching though her brain, she felt better.

Because Grant's arms were exactly what she needed to shelter her from the pain of being abandoned.

Again.

Chapter Two

Grant couldn't remember the last time he'd had a real hangover. Maybe never. Even in college he'd been too focused to ever let loose and party hard. His brothers often told him he was too uptight and needed to relax. And yeah, maybe he was. But he liked being in control. He liked knowing exactly who he was and where he was 24/7.

But even though he knew all that about himself, the heavy-limbed sensation he was feeling, along with the headache that pounded at his temples and the lethargy that had hold of his entire body, had all the markings of the hangover from hell. For a moment he considered not opening his eyes for a while and letting sleep do its job. The big bed was comfortable, after all. A few hours, he figured. Then a shower. A change of clothes. And food when his rolling stomach allowed it. That was the sensible course of action. And he was nothing if not sensible.

And he would have done it, if at that precise moment he hadn't realized that he wasn't alone in the bed. He turned his head a little, ignored the pounding that now traveled to the base of his skull and pried his eyes open a fraction.

Right...

A woman lay on the other side of the huge bed, on her side, her glorious black hair spilling down her naked back. Grant's eyes opened a little more and he admired the smooth skin, catching himself where the sheet lay draped across the curve of her hip. She was asleep, he registered, listening to the soft rhythm of her breathing for a moment.

Recognition fluttered through his brain, and he tried to remember who he was with and what they had done. Images flashed, of skin on skin, of kissing and touching, of sex that was out of this world. The memory made him wince, and the hellish hangover went a couple of rounds in his head. He glanced around the room and then back to the sleeping woman. She stirred, moaning a little, and then rolled, taking the sheet with her as she moved to face him, and he instantly reeled back in shock.

Holy freaking hell... Winnie!

Grant's already addled brain went into overdrive

and then his libido did a leap when he noticed her breasts were bare and were so close he only had to move a few inches and he could…

Snap out of it!

Because…well…what the hell was he doing in bed with *Winnie*?

For one, they were both naked. And the sheets were messed up. And her mouth was full and red and the pinkish mark on her neck looked suspiciously like a love bite.

He spotted a couple of empty bottles of champagne on the table near the window and lifted his head a little to notice other things—like his suit and shoes scattered on the floor and a wedding dress draped over the back of a chair.

More images bombarded him, settling in his memory banks, and he remembered fractured events of the past eighteen hours. Arriving in Vegas. Seeing Winnie in her wedding gown in the foyer and his jaw almost dropping to his feet. Waiting in the chapel. The marine bailing on her. And then…she was crying. He remembered holding her, he remembered offering her words of comfort, he remembered telling her everything would be okay.

And then he quickly remembered other things—like doing way too much drinking. He also remembered being in her hotel room. And then he remembered kissing her, touching her, doing a whole lot of things with her he'd certainly never done be-

fore. He remembered the way she'd felt in his arms—
her eagerness, the pleasure of her touch, the soft sighs
she uttered against his mouth in between kisses. The
way their bodies had moved together. He remembered the heat, the sweat, the desire that had taken
hold of them both for so many hours.

He tried not to look at her and failed. Because it
was impossible to ignore the fact her lips were red-
der than usual, or that her hair was cascading over
her shoulders and back, or the pinkish marks along
her collarbone and neck that looked like a beard rash.
He touched his jaw and felt the culprit, letting out a
long groan. The sound was enough to stir her a little
more and he watched, mesmerized, as she stretched,
moaned and then opened her brown eyes.

She stared at him, adjusting her sight to the morning light beaming through the spot at the window
where the drapes didn't fully meet. And she instantly
jerked back when she noticed him, tugging the sheet
up to cover herself.

"Grant?" She said his name in an almost bloodcurdling whisper. "What… I don't…"

He swallowed hard, unable to move. "Winnie…
we should probably…you know, get up."

She nodded and inched away, taking the sheet
with her. Grant grabbed the duvet at the end of the
bed and covered himself before she got far off the
mattress. Not that it mattered, he supposed, since
he was pretty sure she'd seen everything there was

to see. Because, as much as he didn't want to admit it, there was no hiding the fact that they had spent the night together.

"Oh, my God," she breathed and stumbled from the bed, taking two steps back once her feet hit the floor. "What did we do?"

"I think that's pretty obvious," he replied, trying to not sound as mortified as he felt, and also ignoring the way the sheet slipped down a little, exposing her breasts again. He looked away for a moment while she adjusted the sheet and wrapped the duvet around his waist as he stood, almost falling back onto the bed as the room spun and he swayed.

Great.

"We drank champagne," she said and motioned to the empty bottles on the table. "Lots of it. And tequila."

Grant put a hand to his temple. "Way too much. I never drink like that."

She walked a few paces and then slumped into a chair, keeping the sheet tightly wrapped around herself. She was breathing hard, as though every time she inhaled it actually pained her. She looked up, meeting his gaze, her brown eyes darker than he'd ever seen them, the deeply slanting brows above them adding to the query in her expression. She was beautiful, that's for sure. Her Brazilian heritage had gifted her smooth olive skin, a mane of riotous dark hair, deep chocolate-colored eyes and striking features. She was smart and stunning and had inherited her quick temper from her grandfather. But in that moment, she looked so vulnerable and unsure he was lost for words.

"We had sex," she said, clearly horrified by the idea.

He sighed, then winced a little as his head throbbed. "We did. But it'll be okay, Winnie."

"How is it going to be okay?" she shot back. "We crossed a line."

It was true…they had. The one line that he suspected they both believed they would never cross because they were best friends and that was *way* more important that hooking up for a night of casual sex. And not that it was casual, either…because it was Winnie and they were more than a simple meaningless hookup.

Which meant one thing…*complicated.*

"Winnie, we can move on from this. Last night was…" His words trailed off and he saw the way her eyes glistened. "It doesn't change anything between us."

"Are you kidding?" she shot back quickly. "It changes everything."

"Only if we let it," he added. "And we won't, okay?"

She shook her head. "Sex complicates everything."

"Not for us," he said, trying to put her at ease, despite knowing she was right. And despite the way his stomach churned and his brain felt like it was about to explode. "Our friendship is unbreakable."

She didn't look convinced. "I think I'm going to throw up." Their eyes clashed and she shrugged. "From the alcohol, I mean. Not from…" She waved a hand as her words trailed off. "You know…*that*."

He was stupidly pleased to hear it. For one, this was Winnie and he hated to think he'd done anything to hurt or offend her. And two, he had as much ego as the next guy. He looked at her, noticing everything, the way she bit down on her lower lip, the way her naked shoulders were held tight, the way her tousled hair looked as sexy as hell.

Sexy… Jesus…what the hell is wrong with me?

He shook himself and took a breath, trying to ignore the snapshot of images toying with his brain. Memories of kissing her, of touching her in places he'd never dared imagine he would touch, of lying between her thighs and being inside her in the most intimate way possible. And then, as the images gained momentum and he experienced a deep-rooted churning way down low, Grant noticed something else—a gold band shimmering on her left hand.

"Ah… Winnie," he said, the words almost collapsing his throat. "You're wearing a wedding ring."

She looked down and gasped, her face turning ghostly pale. She shot her gaze back to his as she held up her hand. Her gaze didn't waver from his for a few excruciating seconds and then she tilted her head to the side and glanced down.

"Oh, my God," she whispered and jumped to her feet, pointing to his left hand. "So are you, Grant!"

His lids dropped and he looked to where his left hand was clutching the slipping duvet. Holy crap! She was right. The bright gold band on his ring finger was plain to see.

No...it couldn't be...

He searched his memory banks, trying to remember, pulling on his recall...and slowly, piece by piece, the fragments began to merge. They'd been at the chapel, Winnie was upset, crying over the jerk who'd dumped her. Grant had her in his arms, holding her, soothing her, telling her how everything would be okay. And then later, they were at the hotel, back in the bistro and drinking a pitcher of mojitos. After that they had done a few rounds of tequila shots. She'd cried some more, then once her bravado set in, began to curse her ex-fiancé, using words he'd never heard her speak before. They walked the strip for a while, laughing, arm in arm, stopping at another bar for a drink and a bowl of pretzels. And then, somehow, they were back at the chapel.

Do you take this woman...

To have and to hold....

'Til death do you part...

The memories banged around in his head. Taunting him, awakening feelings he wasn't sure he knew what to do with. Feelings he didn't want. Because he didn't do feelings—not these, that was for damn sure.

He strode three steps across the room and snatched up a couple of pieces of paper that were on the table by the window. He looked at the documents, scanning them quickly, and the uneasiness in his gut increased as the seconds passed. He saw names, signatures, a blurry stamp in dark ink...and he knew exactly what he was looking at.

A marriage license.

His name. Winnie's name. Two signatures he recognized in the bride and groom section, and a couple he didn't were scrawled in the witness section. It was undeniable. Unimaginable.

They were married.

"We've got a situation," he said quietly, glancing at her and then looking at the damning document in his hands. "It looks like we got hitched last night."

Color leached from her face and he could see that her hands were shaking.

"That's impossible," she said, almost croaking out the words.

He shook his head and then took a few steps across the room, holding out the paper in his hand. "Take a look."

She grabbed the page and the crackling sound reverberated in his ears, reminding him of the headache and hangover he was so desperately trying to forget he had. He wanted some aspirin, a shower, shave and coffee in that order. Grant looked around the room and spotted his clothes and shoes.

The bridal suite, he figured, taking in the over-the-top decor and huge bed.

The marriage bed.

Where they had foolishly consummated their union. Damn…the situation quickly spiraled from bad to worse when he realized what that meant. Married *and* lovers. Which made the idea of annulment unlikely, right? Which of course is what they would do. Winnie wouldn't want to be married to him any more than he wanted to be married to her. Hell, he didn't want to be married to anyone.

"How could we let this happen?" she said as she scanned the page and then thrust it back into his hands. "Yesterday I was…"

Dreaming of marrying someone else…

Oddly, the notion irked him and he couldn't understand why. Sure, he didn't think the marine was good enough for her and believed they should know one another better, but that didn't mean he wanted to step into the other man's shoes. But he had…in every way possible.

He let out a weary sigh. "Well… I guess we'll have to get a divorce."

Winona had never been more confused in her life. Twenty-four hours ago her plans had been set—

marry Dwight, move to California, start her new life with her new husband.

Oh, yeah…she had a husband, all right…just not the one she'd planned on!

Winona Culhane…

Simply thinking the words made her head hurt. And her heart hurt, too.

She looked at Grant, absorbing every inch of him in a microsecond. Naked from the waist up, the duvet wrapped haphazardly low on his waist, he looked as sexy as sin. His broad shoulders were smooth and tanned, his chest covered in a light dusting of hair that tapered down his belly and disappeared beneath the duvet. Of course she'd seen him shirtless before. But never like this. Never after sex. She considered the way her body felt, the ache in the backs of her thighs and the heavy lethargy seeping through to her bones, and the haze her brain seemed to be in. She'd had two other lovers in her twenty-six years—her high school boyfriend and Dwight. Casual sex had never interested her.

But Grant, she knew, only did casual.

He'd never had a long-term relationship. A couple of months and he was out. She knew the drill. He'd meet someone, they would date, she wouldn't move into his apartment—as far as Winona knew, he wouldn't even let a toothbrush be left at his place. He wasn't a player and never cheated in his relationships, but he wasn't exactly known for going the distance.

And yet, here they were—married!

The nausea returned, clutching at her throat, and she put a hand to her mouth. The last thing she wanted to do was throw up in front of him—that would be too humiliating. She had to get a grip, to prove she was in control and able to deal with their current situation.

"Divorce?" She repeated his suggestion and stared at him, not wanting to think about how much she was stung by his quick solution. "Why not an annulment?"

He raised both brows and pointed to the rumpled bed. "Er...not that I'm an expert on South Dakota's marriage laws, but I think we may have botched that option when we...you know...spent the night together."

Winona's insides crunched up. She didn't know how to feel or what to think.

She walked across the room, clutching the sheet, passing him without taking a breath as she headed for the bathroom. She closed the door and pressed her back against the wall, the cold tiles making her wince a little. Winona took a couple of long breaths and then stared into the long mirror.

Oh, my God... I look wrecked.

Her hair was everywhere, her eyes bloodshot, her grayish pallor indicative of way too much alcohol consumed. She jumped in the shower for a couple of minutes, washing quickly, ignoring the throbbing sensation at the back of her head. Aspirin would be good, she figured, and once she'd dried off and wrapped the sheet back around herself, she rummaged through her toiletries for the painkillers. She found them, took two, left another couple on the washbasin and then opened the door. Grant was still standing by the bed, still draped in a duvet, still looking so hot she had to swallow a couple of times to get her lady parts out of the way of her brain so she could stop remembering, thinking and fantasizing about her new husband in any way whatsoever!

Because she loved Dwight, right? At least, she *had* loved him until he dumped her so heartlessly and left her standing at the altar. Of course, she hated him, too, since he had no right to treat her so badly. This time yesterday she had been dreaming of her wedding and her new life. Now, she was living an actual nightmare—with a seminaked Grant playing center stage as her husband!

"We should get dressed," she said flatly, searching for her suitcase among the discarded clothes on the floor. "I left some aspirin for you in the bathroom."

She found her suitcase by the window, opened, and her belongings a jumbled mess.

"What?" he asked, obviously noticing her scrunched-up expression.

"I can't believe we did this."

"Which part?" he remarked. "The drinking, the wedding, the—"

"All of it," she snapped, cutting him off. "Yesterday..."

"Yesterday your idiot ex-fiancé abandoned you. You needed to forget about it *and* him. That's why we—"

"It's no excuse," she said quickly, rummaging through her bag for suitable clothing. She found jeans, fresh underwear and a red shirt and pulled them into her arms. "We've got to fix this."

"Of course," he said quickly. "Once we get home I'll go and see Tyler Madden. He'll know the best course of action."

Tyler Madden was a lawyer in Cedar River. Winona had met him briefly when he'd looked after her grandfather's will.

"I'd like to get dressed," she said quietly. "You can have the bathroom."

He hesitated for a moment, as though he wanted to say something, but instead he nodded. "Sure," he said and grabbed his clothes and shoes, struggling to hold the duvet with one hand. "Good idea."

He disappeared quickly and Winona relaxed a fraction. She used the sheet as a makeshift tent as she wobbled on her feet, slipping into her underwear and jeans. She remained on point, dropping the sheet for a few moments, her gaze fixed firmly on the bathroom door as she thrust her arms into her shirt and quickly did up the row of buttons. She found her shoes and then gathered up her scattered clothing, taking a second to look over the crumpled wedding gown. A few of the pearl buttons were missing and she remembered the way she'd rushed to get out of the dress in her eagerness to have sex with Grant, the way she'd clung to him, begged him, kissed him like she was starved of touch. And was instantly mortified by the memory. She was a predictable cliché…a woman who'd pounced on her best friend the moment she'd needed a rebound lay. Appalled, she rolled the gown up and pushed it into the suitcase, along with shoes and anything else she found on the floor.

He emerged from the bathroom a few minutes later, dressed in his suit, his jaw still raspy with a five-o'clock shadow. She tried not to stare, keeping herself busy by unzipping and then rezipping her bag.

"My plane leaves at 10:40," he said and tossed the duvet in the middle of the bed. "Would you like me to arrange a flight for you? I'm guessing you don't want to hang around here for any longer than necessary?"

That was true. Winona had a flight booked for Monday. It was now Friday morning—she certainly didn't want to be alone in Vegas for three days, pacing around the honeymoon suite, her mind a mix of memories, thinking about Dwight *or* Grant. She rummaged through her bag and pulled out her airplane ticket.

"Thank you," she said and passed him the ticket.

"I'm gonna head back to my room for a shower and change of clothes. I'll be back soon."

She didn't say anything else and waited until he was gone before she sighed and managed to relax a little. She made coffee and drank it as hot as she could stand, and paced the room until he returned about twenty minutes later, carrying his overnight bag.

"We're all set for our flight," he said, unsmiling. "And the concierge has arranged for a car to take us to the airport at nine. We have time for breakfast in the restaurant downstairs. Or we could order room service."

Winona glanced at the clock on the wall: 7:50. The last thing she wanted was to be cooped up in a room with Grant for the following hour. "Downstairs," she said and picked up her suitcase and handbag, sweeping the room one last time for anything she might have left behind, before she collected her toiletries from the bathroom.

She glanced down at her hand and realized she still wore the wedding band. She looked at his hand and noticed it was bare, thinking that removing it was probably the first thing he'd done when he got to his room. She met Grant's gaze and let out a long sigh. "I should take this off."

The ring came off easily and she dropped it into the small pocket inside her tote. Shame pushed down on her shoulders again and she swallowed back the tightness in her throat. She wanted to cry, but absolutely would not fall apart in front of him.

"Let's go," she said flatly and walked from the room.

Once they were downstairs, they left their bags with the concierge and headed for the restaurant. There were plenty of tables free and Winona was relieved to see it was a buffet-style arrangement—it meant she had time to linger by the buffet table and avoid sitting down with him for any length of time. She piled up her plate with fruit and toast and headed for their table, conscious that Grant was still selecting his food. She poured herself a glass of water, drank it in a few seconds and then poured another, grateful that the aspirin she'd taken earlier was now kicking in.

By the time he sat down at their table she was struggling to digest a second piece of cantaloupe and looked up. It was time to get serious about their situation. "So, we need to make a pact," she said and grabbed a napkin.

He looked at her. "A what?"

"Pact," she repeated. "Agreement. Arrangement. You know, a pact."

"About?"

"To not tell anyone what we've done."

"Which part?" he queried, one brow up.

"The married part," she replied as heat crawled up her neck. "The sex part. Promise me."

"Of course," he said quickly and sipped coffee. "But you know what my family is like, Winnie, and I hate the idea of keeping secrets from them."

"Sometimes secrets are necessary," she said.

"Don't I know it," he shot back.

Winona stared at him. "What does that mean?"

He shook his head dismissively. "Nothing."

"Perhaps we should get a lawyer in Rapid City. You've lived there for years, surely you know someone?"

He pushed his untouched plate away. "Maybe. You know Len Pearson—he got divorced last year, so I could ask him."

Winona knew all of Grant's friends, including Len, who she didn't particularly like. "It will probably be easier just to go and see Tyler, then. He's a good lawyer and we'll just need to make sure we're discreet. And we should deal with it before word gets out. I don't want anyone knowing about this."

"Winnie, I don't think—"

"I feel so ashamed I can barely breathe," she admitted as she cut off his words, holding her shoulders so tight her bones ached.

He exhaled heavily. "I do understand how you—"

"No, you couldn't possibly," she said, cutting him off again. "Just yesterday I was going to marry the man I loved and start my new life and now it's all—"

"Loved?" he questioned, both brows now up. "You said that in the past tense. So, what…you don't love him anymore?"

"How could I possibly—after what he did to me?"

"If that's all it took, then his leaving you at the altar was clearly the best thing for you both."

Winona glared at him. "How dare you say that. What do you know about anything? Your idea of a real relationship is allowing your date to order dessert."

He scowled, clearly stung by her words. "At least I have sense enough not to marry someone I haven't seen for the last ten months."

It was a cruel dig and one she didn't deserve. Grant knew how much her relationship with Dwight meant to her—since she spoke to him about it most nights when they talked on the phone.

She met his gaze. "Why are you being like this?"

He sighed heavily. "Because I'm tired, and when I'm tired I act like a jerk. Sorry."

"You're right, though," she admitted and shrugged. "I was clearly not thinking straight when I agreed to marry Dwight. And what was last night if not a complete lapse in judgment?" she added a little hotly, so annoyed with herself she could hardly breathe. "We got drunk, got married and had sex… I'd say as far as lapses go, that's the lapse of the century."

He laughed. "I don't think I've ever been called that before."

"It's not funny," she retorted. "This is the worst day of my life. Which is a strange irony, because it should have been the best day. I've done some foolish things over the years, but I've never had rebound sex before, have you?"

"Is that what it was?" he asked quietly, looking

at her over the rim of his cup, his gaze unbeliev-
ably intense.

"Of course, what else?"

He shrugged, but Winona saw the tension in his
shoulders. She suspected he was acting cool because
he thought it was better for them both, but she knew
him too well—she knew he was faking. He wasn't
cool, he wasn't okay, he was as wound up, as confused, as completely out of sorts, as she was. He
was simply better at disguising it. He was the master of it, in fact.

"Can't you just admit that you're as freaked out
about this as I am?" she challenged him.

His gaze didn't waver. "Would it change anything?"

"For starters," she said and huffed, "it might stop
me being mad at you for acting like the Tin Man."

"Well, we're certainly not in Kansas anymore,"
he replied and drank some more coffee and then
checked his watch. "We should get going."

Relief scored down her back. "Great idea."

Winona got to her feet and pushed the chair in,
grabbing her tote. She was halfway around the table
when Grant grasped her hand. She felt the connection. The burn. The tingle his touch always evoked.
And any other time she wouldn't have thought anything of it—like when they were at the movies and
he led her to their seats, or if they were out to dinner
and he pulled out her chair, or if they were dancing,

or if they were mustering cattle at the ranch and he helped her mount her tall gelding. But this wasn't any other time. This was now. They were married. They were lovers. And everything was different.

She pulled away, weirdly missing his touch the second their fingertips were apart.

In that moment she knew why she was so over-wrought; it wasn't because Dwight had dumped her. It was much, much worse.

It was because she was terrified that, amid it all, she'd lost her best friend.

Chapter Three

Back in Cedar River late that afternoon, Winona imagined things might be better. But they weren't. After an awkward flight, she and Grant had parted at the airport in Rapid City with barely a goodbye as they headed toward their cars, both parked in the long-term parking lot.

Now, she was curled up on her sofa, a mug of green tea pressed between her palms, staring through the window of her one-bedroom apartment above the bakery. The sweet scent of sugar and cinnamon from that morning's bake still lingered in the air and gave her some comfort. She'd lived in the apartment for a few years, and mostly enjoyed the solitude. She had a few friends in town, like Grant's sister, Ellie, and his cousin Leah, but since Grant was her closest friend, most of her spare socializing time was spent with him.

Not anymore...

The terse way they had parted company at the airport made things abundantly clear—after almost twenty years of friendship, their relationship was forever changed.

And it hurt...in some ways, more than Dwight bailing on their wedding. Of course she was deeply wounded by her fiancé's behavior, but she realized now she'd get over it. She was strong, resilient. She'd been left before and survived. This, however, was something else. Grant had said they were unbreakable, but she wasn't so sure. He'd always been there to help her through tough times—but how could he help her through *this*? How could they help each other?

She didn't understand how things had taken such a turn, and after the drama of the past couple of days, she was too emotionally drained to figure out just what in the hell they'd been thinking when they'd exchanged vows—and ended up in bed.

If Dwight had shown up, things would have been very different. She'd be on her honeymoon. She wouldn't be broken inside. But maybe she *was* really better off, since Dwight obviously didn't want to marry her. Maybe he never had.

She got to her feet around six and changed into a

pair of shorts and an old green T-shirt and then un-packed her suitcase. The crumpled wedding gown was quickly shoved into a garment bag and hung up at the back of the closet, and the matching shoes received similar treatment. She piled the laundry in the hamper and then headed to the kitchen. She ate a noodle cup standing at the countertop, took some more aspirin for the lingering headache and was back on the sofa by eight o'clock.

Noise from the street below filtered through the open windows, mostly people walking toward JoJo's pizza place down the block. Laughter echoed and she experienced a deep sense of loneliness through to her bones. Lately, it seemed as though loneliness was a frequent companion. Silly, she supposed, when she had her grandfather and Ellie and the rest of the Culhanes in town. And yet, it was that hunger for company that had drawn her toward Dwight, wasn't it? He was nice and friendly and low maintenance as a boyfriend—since he lived in another state and was then stationed overseas. Winona wondered if that's exactly why she had started their relationship in the first place. He'd been physically absent from her life for the most part, which meant she didn't have to invest much of herself.

On reflection, it wasn't a particularly flattering picture.

Her phone rang and she looked at the number. *Grant.*

She picked up on the fifth ring, after several agonizing seconds considering letting it go to messages. "Hello."

"Hey," he said after a second's pause. "How are you?"

"Fine," she replied. "You?"

"Same," he said and then sighed. "I was worried about you."

"Like I said," she remarked, her throat tightening. "I'm fine. And actually just about to make it an early night."

He was silent for a few long seconds. "Winnie," he said, his voice so soft she pressed the phone closer to her ear. "I hate this. We've never had trouble talking, not ever."

"We've never been married before, either," she reminded him. "So, I'm not sure the usual rules apply."

He expelled an exasperated breath. "Can't we just… I don't know…move on from this?"

His ability to compartmentalize their relationship so easily both infuriated and hurt her. "Do you mean before or after the divorce?"

Another sigh. "You're being difficult, you know that, right?"

"I'm being realistic. You're acting as though nothing has changed. As though this doesn't mean anything."

"Of course it means something," he said quickly.

"But, Winnie, does it have to mean *everything*? Can't we just get past it and move on?"

Winona sucked in a breath. He didn't get it.

"Good night, Grant," she said impatiently.

"Winnie…don't…"

"I'm not like you, Grant… I can't just switch off my feelings."

"I don't do that," he said, his tone lowering an octave.

"Sure you do," she replied. "That's how you've managed to avoid loving anyone your whole life."

He was silent and she knew she'd hit a nerve. Her own nerves rattled, too. Because talking about Grant loving someone made her insides ache in a way she'd avoided thinking about for years.

"I don't…*not love*…people," he said, and she heard his voice crack a little.

"I don't mean your brothers or your sister or even…" Her words trailed off for a moment and she swallowed hard. "Or even me. I only mean…" She stalled again, desperate to backpedal. "I mean…you know…you've never really had a serious relationship."

"Like yours and the marine?" he asked. "Is that what you mean?"

Heat surged through her. "Actually, I don't know what I mean. I'm tired and I need to get some sleep. I'll talk to you tomorrow."

He sighed. "Sure. Good night, Winnie."

She ended the call and swallowed back a sob. It was the first time in forever that they'd ended their conversation in such a way. There was no saying *I love ya*. There was no *Ditto*. There was nothing but thick, relentless tension.

Winona turned in around nine o'clock and spent several hours staring at the ceiling. Her bedroom had one window that overlooked the street and she left the curtains open so she could see the colors from the traffic lights below. The changing hues were oddly comforting as she endeavored to drift off to sleep. She woke up at seven and puttered around the apartment doing a few chores and, at eight, dressed in jeans, shirt and light jacket and headed downstairs.

The bakery was busy and she slipped through the rear entrance, waving to the three women behind the counter. The owner, Regina Drake, was clearing tables as she talked to patrons and Winona smiled as she waited in line for service. The other woman had purchased the bakery about two years earlier and they had become quite friendly over that time. Winona even helped out occasionally, when one of the staff called in sick. It was a busy change from her regular job doing admin at the tourist center in town.

She ordered a latte and her favorite bagel to go and was waiting for her order when she saw Grant striding through the entrance. Of course he knew her usual Saturday routine.

"Hey there," he said and shrugged when he reached her. "How'd you sleep?"

"Lousy," she admitted, trying not to look at him. "You?"

"About the same," he replied and quickly ordered a black coffee. "I stared at the ceiling for most of the night and gave up around five-thirty. I went for a run," he said, not quite looking at her. "And then I thought I'd try and meet you here for breakfast."

"I'm getting mine to go," she said, looking as unenthused as she could.

He gazed at her for a moment, then asked, "Winnie, is every conversation we have from now on going to be a hard one?" He was frowning a little.

"Maybe. Look, I need some time to digest things," she said.

"Well, how about we digest things over breakfast," he suggested.

Winona shot him a skeptical look. "Black coffee isn't breakfast."

"I had a protein shake earlier and that's all I can stomach," he admitted. "I'm still recovering from the champagne and tequila the other night."

She wasn't surprised. He rarely drank and was very health conscious, having been a vegetarian since he was fifteen. She knew he worked out at the gym several days a week and ran three miles every morning. He traveled a lot for his job, which was mostly sedentary, but certainly kept himself in shape.

"You should eat something," she found herself saying. "Food is good for a hangover."

His brow rose. "Only if you'll stay and keep me company for a while."

Her order arrived and she relented, finding a quiet table in the corner of the bakery. She sat, spooned a little sugar into her latte and waited for him to join her, carrying his coffee and a muffin on a plate. She looked him over as he approached—in dark, low-rise jeans, a gray twill shirt and cowboy boots, he looked sexy and wholly masculine—and her heart skipped a couple of beats. Winona knew she was foolish, but couldn't help herself. Green eyes, dark brown hair, a strong, square jaw—she couldn't help but find him attractive!

He sat down and pulled in the chair, resting his elbows on the table. "I thought we could hang out and talk for a while."

"Great," she said with fake enthusiasm. "What would you like to talk about?"

He chuckled and the sound hit her directly behind the ribs. She really did need to pull herself together. With her resolve galvanized, Winona stared at him, one brow up, waiting for his response.

Which didn't come, because Regina approached their table and laid a hand on his shoulder. Winona pushed back the surge of green-eyed monster and took a breath. As far as she knew, Regina was madly in love with her longtime musician boyfriend and

wasn't the sort to covet another woman's husband…
even if that husband was a huge secret and an even
bigger mistake!

"Hey, you two," Regina said. "Isn't it beautiful out
there today? Grant, you seem like a persuasive sort
of guy—see if you can finally get Winnie to agree to
come into partnership with me, will you?"

It was a long-standing conversation between them—
Regina wanted a partner so she could step back a little
from the business and spend more time having a per-
sonal life. Winona wasn't totally against the idea—in
fact, she was sorely tempted. She simply didn't have
the funds to cover the investment. Her job at the tourist center just didn't afford her the luxury of saving
a large nest egg once her rent and utilities were paid
each month, and she wasn't prepared to borrow the
money from a bank or any other avenue. Including
Grant, who'd offered several times to loan her the
money. Truth be told, he'd *give* it to her in a heartbeat
if she asked.

"I'll see what I can do," he said and grinned, waiting until Regina headed off before speaking again.
"You know, it's not a bad idea. You've been saying
for ages how bored you are with your job."

"Which doesn't mean I'm going to jump into a
risky business venture," she countered, sipping her
latte.

He looked around the busy bakery for a moment.
"Looks like a pretty safe investment, though. And

I'm sure Regina would be a good business partner.
Sometimes you have to take a leap of faith."

She laughed. "That's rich, coming from Mr. Über-
cautious-About-Everything."

He scowled. "I'm not like that."

"Ha," she flipped back, "you're as predictable as
the sun setting every night."

"No," he countered. "I don't think so."

Winona raised both brows and began counting
off her fingers. "One, you go running every morning at 6:15. Not ten past six, or twenty past six, but
6:15 precisely. Two, you own half a dozen pale blue
shirts and team them with a darker shade blue tie and
wear that to work every day—no exceptions. I know
this because I have given you three or four humorous
ties over the years and you've never worn them." She
counted on another finger. "Three, you stir your coffee five times counterclockwise. Four, you've used
the same cologne for the last decade. Shall I go on?"

"What, because I like blue shirts and can stick
to my schedule and wake up in time to go running
every morning, that makes me predictable?"

"Yep," she replied, enjoying his scowl. "You
wouldn't take a risk if your life depended on it."

It came out sounding like an insult, as though
she was making some huge character judgment and
found him lacking. Which, of course, was ridiculous.
She loved the fact he was predictable and calm and
rock solid. It's why she had gravitated toward him

when they were kids. He knew who he was, what he wanted, where he was going. At sixteen he'd begun planning his future career, at eighteen he'd gone to college and at twenty-one got his first job in program design. Now, he flew across the west coast for his work. He was well regarded in his field, highly sought after and very good at what he did. Whereas, most days, Winona felt like a complete failure in the career department.

"Sorry. I didn't mean to come off like that. You know what I mean," she said and sighed. "You've always known who you are and what you wanted. Not like me," she added and made a face.

"You just haven't figured out what you want to do for a career," he said quietly. "That's not a crime. It takes time to figure out what makes you happy."

She knew he was right, and she also knew she needed to make some changes. She'd studied history in college before switching to an undeclared major after a couple of semesters, knowing the subject wasn't for her. After her grandfather had his last stroke, he was diagnosed with Parkinson's disease, and Winona decided to take time off from school to make him a priority. At first she'd moved back into their cabin, but eventually she felt he was strong enough for her to find a place of her own in town. He'd supported her moving from the Triple C Ranch, knowing she needed her own life independent of the Culhanes, but he was happy to stay on the ranch and live out his days there. She helped out on the ranch when she could, during mustering and branding seasons, and often assisted Mitch with the horse breaking and training. Her job at the tourist center was simply a way of paying her bills—certainly not her dream job.

"When I said you were predictable and wouldn't know how to take a risk, I didn't mean it to sound like I was criticizing you," she said and took a sharp breath.

"I'm pretty sure no one would have predicted that we'd get married," he said quietly, his voice so low she inched forward in her seat to hear him.

But suddenly she didn't want to talk anymore; she didn't want to talk about their nuptials or impending divorce. And she didn't want to think about the other thing, which was raging like a giant red flag between them.

Sex...

They'd crossed a line. There was no going back.

Grant had spent the last twenty-four hours in a kind of daze. He knew he and Winnie needed to talk, but she wasn't making it easy. He also knew she was upset, hurt and probably embarrassed by what had transpired over the past couple of days. He'd experienced most of those feelings himself in one form or another.

The thing was, he didn't know how to talk to her when she was in such a bad mood.

He also didn't want to keep thinking about her in the way he was.

Because now that his memory was clear, he remembered the sensational sex they'd had. He remembered how she'd responded to his touch and the memories were acute, distracting him from the issue at hand—namely, their impromptu wedding and the quick need for a divorce. He'd do as he promised—arrange for them to see a lawyer on Monday and try and get the whole thing straightened out as soon as possible. In the meantime, though, he wanted to make sure Winona was okay about what had happened between them. Especially before he had to take off again for work. He was flying to San Francisco on Wednesday.

"Are you staying in town for the weekend?" she asked.

"I was thinking I would. Mitch is always nagging me to come home more often. I'm sure there'll be the usual family gathering at the ranch this weekend."

She shrugged. "I planned on seeing my grandfather this morning, but I'm not sure I want to face a crowd. He might want to talk about Dwight and I don't think I'm up for it."

"You'll have to tell your grandfather that the marine is out of the picture at some point," he remarked. "Better sooner than later."

She sighed heavily. "I suppose so."

"You don't have to say anything else," Grant said quietly. "Just that you guys broke up."

"I guess I don't," she said on a sigh. "No one needs to know I was dumped at the altar, right?"

"No, they don't," he replied, feeling the twitch in his gut sharpen because she looked so unhappy and he knew he was part of the reason for her mood. Sure, the marine had a lot to answer for, and in the cold light of day Grant was sorely tempted to contact the other man and have it out with him for being such a jerk. "You'll get through this. You're stronger than you think," he assured her. "We're not the first people to make a mistake, Winnie, and we won't be the last. We just have to get through it. And we can."

"Can we?" she queried, her eyes huge, the irises turning a deep chocolate brown.

He reached across the table and grasped her hand. Something he'd done countless times before. She resisted, not quite pulling away, but looking like his touch was the last thing she wanted. The twitch in his gut increased and he gently closed his fingers around hers. "Sure we can."

"I don't have your confidence," she said quietly, moving her hand away and tucking it in her lap. "The thing is, any other time, any other situation, you'd be the person I wanted to talk to if I was feeling like this."

"Then talk to me," he insisted.

"I can't," she said and pushed back the chair, her eyes glittering. "I'm so appalled and embarrassed and…disappointed. In Dwight and in myself and in…"

Her words trailed off, but he got her meaning. "In me, you mean? Believe me, Winnie, if I could undo the last couple of days, I would."

The glittering in her eyes turned into tears and he fought the battle he had going on in his head— the one that instinctively made him long to soothe her, to be the balm for her pain and hurt. It's what he'd always done. What *they'd* always done for one another. Until now.

"You can't," she said dully. "This one isn't an easy fix, Grant. This one includes lawyers and divorce, and the very idea of that makes me sick to my stomach. Instead of marrying the man who proposed to me, I find myself married to a man who's acting as though this situation is just a blip on the radar, something we can pretend never happened. Well, it's more than that to me. Because it *did* happen. It happened to *us*, Grant," she implored, tears on her cheeks. "And I know you think we can get past this, but I don't share your confidence."

She walked away, leaving her untouched breakfast on the table. Grant watched as she slipped behind the counter and headed upstairs. He considered following her and then abandoned the idea. He left the café and walked to his car, which was parked outside. He drove slowly down Main Street and headed for the highway.

The trip to the ranch took about twenty minutes and as he drove through the gates he relaxed a little. It was home. Regardless of where he lived, the ranch and everything on it reminded him of who he was and where he came from. Culhanes had lived on the Triple C for generations and the ranch was in good hands under Mitch's guidance. His oldest brother was honest and hardworking, a man who'd put his own life on hold at eighteen so he could take guardianship of his five younger siblings. Without Mitch, they would have been forced to leave the ranch and been farmed out through social services. But Mitch would never have allowed that. Even now, nearly twenty years later, his brother was the glue that held the family together.

He spotted his brother coming out of the house the moment he pulled up. The quintessential cowboy, Mitch's familiar swagger made him smile. Grant liked horses well enough and helped around the ranch when he could, but the life wasn't ingrained in his DNA like it was with Mitch.

His brother greeted him with a bear hug. "It's good to see you. Tess and I were just talking about you last night."

"You were?" Grant queried. Tess was Mitch's wife. They'd been married once before, got divorced, then reconnected again a couple of years ago. Now they had a son, Charlie, and were happily remarried and thoroughly in love. It was a complicated story, but Grant was pleased they had managed to work through their troubles.

"We were hoping you'd come for a visit this weekend," Mitch said as Grant grabbed his bag from the trunk. "Joss and the girls will be here soon. Sissy is having trouble with an assignment for her computer science class and Ellie was going to give her a hand with it. But now you're here," Mitch said and grinned, "all the better."

Grant had always been the geek in the family. "Sure, no problem."

They entered the house and Grant was filled with a heavy sense of melancholy. It always hit him, every time he came home. Memories, both good and bad, bombarded his thoughts, no doubt amplified by Billie-Jack's recent message—a complication he didn't have the head space to think about, not when he had so much going on with Winnie.

Tess greeted them in the hallway and gave him an affectionate hug, pulling him from his thoughts.

"Where's my nephew?" he asked and returned the embrace.

"Napping," she replied and exhaled. "Poor little guy has his last couple of teeth coming through, so we've had a few sleepless nights." Tess eyed him curiously. "Everything okay with you?"

"Sure," he lied. Tess was an intuitive woman and

he suspected that if he didn't pull himself together she'd figure out something was wrong pretty quickly. "Great. Is Ellie around?"

"I think she's in the office at the stables doing a stock feed order," Tess replied. "I was just about to make coffee and put out some of Mrs. B's famous banana-and-walnut loaf."

He grinned. Mrs. Bailey had been the housekeeper on the Triple C for about seventeen years and was considered part of the family, and Grant loved her cooking. She lived in one of four cottages behind the main house. Ellie lived in the largest; Wes, the ranch foreman, lived in another, and Red Sheehan lived in one, while the last was left for guests. Grant had moved from the ranch for college and had never permanently returned, but he liked knowing there was a room upstairs that was his any time he wanted it. His childhood room was now the nursery and he passed it once he headed upstairs. He dumped his bag on the end of the bed in the guest room and walked back downstairs, stopping in the stairway to glance over the family photographs.

Generations of Culhanes stared back at him. His grandparents, Aurora and Henry, and his mom, Louise, who looked so pretty in a blue dress and heels. There was even an old snapshot of Billie-Jack with his arm looped around his mom's waist. Happy times. Back then Grant had worshipped his father. But then Grant's mother had died and Billie-Jack went off the rails. He couldn't handle the loss of his wife, and instead of helping his children cope with their sorrows, he drowned his own in a bottle. Worse—he became an abusive drunk. Jake got the brunt of it, since he would antagonize Billie-Jack so the old man would leave the rest of them alone.

Then, when Grant was twelve, a drunken Billie-Jack drove his truck down an embankment. Grant had been in the back seat, and Hank, two years older, had been in the front beside their father. He remembered Jake tailing them on his motorbike, and how his older brother had pulled Grant out of the truck just before it caught fire. Billie-Jack, not wearing a seat belt, had been flung clear of the burning wreck. But Hank wasn't so lucky and had suffered burns to over twenty percent of his body. Over the next few years, Hank spent most of his time in the burn unit in the Rapid City hospital, enduring countless surgeries and skin grafts.

By then Billie-Jack had bailed. He left them all with Mitch and handed over custody without a fight.

At the time, they'd been stunned—by the painful loss of their mother, and now by the desertion of their father. Looking back, though, Grant realized his leaving was probably the best thing for everyone. Billie-Jack had messed up and didn't deserve the family he'd abandoned. But still, Grant often wondered what life would have been like if his father had resisted his demons and accepted his responsibility to his family.

Maybe they'd all be screwed up. As it was, they'd all turned out okay. Mitch had looked after them. Made sure they all went to school, and that they all stayed together. Now he ran the Triple C and had a family of his own. Jake, who'd gone into the military after high school, had reconciled with his high school sweetheart a year or so back after discovering he had a seven-year-old son. Hank was chief of police in Cedar River. In an eerie echo of his father's experience, Joss was a single dad raising his girls after losing his young wife to cancer. Except that Joss was a wonderful dad. And Ellie still lived on the ranch, helping with the horse-breeding program.

In hindsight, they were lucky Billie-Jack left and Mitch took over. Grant was very grateful his brother sought full custody and then stepped up to raise them. He thought about Billie-Jack and the two calls he'd ignored from the old man in the last few weeks. He thought about what his brother would say—about what *all* his siblings would say—and then decided to keep the information to himself for a while longer. They didn't need to know just yet.

Grant lingered on the stairs for a few more moments before heading downstairs. He walked into the kitchen and chatted to Tess and Mrs. B for a few minutes, then headed through the mudroom and outside. It was a warm and sunny day, and after all the hours he spent at a desk, being outdoors always reenergized him. He considered taking one of the horses out for ride and was halfway into making the decision when his sister, Ellie, emerged from the stables and strode across the yard. As a child she'd been sassy and adorable; now, she was five feet four inches of spirited, redheaded beauty, yet he still loved calling her Brat.

"Where've you been hiding these last couple of days?" she said as she hugged him. "I've left three messages on your cell since Thursday."

He'd gotten the messages, but had been too caught up in other things—namely Winnie. "Sorry—I've been busy."

She frowned. "I need some help with this new DNA mapping system we've started using and Alvarez is breathing down my neck to get all the information input before the end of the month."

Ramon Alvarez was an ex–reigning champion and horse trainer from Arizona who Mitch had gone into partnership with several years ago. Grant suspected Ellie didn't dislike the other man as much as she protested, and happily dissed her about him whenever the chance arose.

"Boyfriend trouble?" he teased.

She made a face. "Spare me. You know very well the only thing I like about him are his horses, that's all."

"I dunno, Brat," he teased again. "You know the old saying about protesting too much?"

Ellie smiled extra sweetly. "Have you seen Win?" she asked and linked her arm through his.

"This morning," he replied, his gut tightening. "Why?"

"She's also been off-grid for the past few days," Ellie replied. "Which isn't like her."

He shrugged vaguely, ignoring the damning *also* in his sister's words. "Maybe she's working."

"Nope," Ellie said. "I checked at the tourist center. And she's not answering my calls, either. How was she when you saw her?"

"The usual," he said and quickly changed the subject. "I thought I'd take one of the horses out while I'm here."

"Take Bianco," she said and grinned. "He hasn't been ridden for a month."

Bianco was a big, bad-tempered overo gelding that bucked everyone off. Him included. Grant had no idea why Mitch didn't sell the animal. "No one can ride that thing."

"Alvarez can," she admitted and scowled again. "The man certainly knows how to ride a horse, I'll give him that."

Grant laughed and felt some of the tension leave his system. The ranch and Ellie were always good medicine. As they walked across the yard, a car appeared coming up the driveway. The classic, bright orange VW was unmistakable.

Winnie…

His insides constricted instantly. He wasn't used to feeling tense around her. It didn't sit right. The car pulled up beside his and she got out, her glorious black hair flowing around her shoulders, her hips swaying as she walked, and the uncharacteristic twitch in his gut amplified, turning into something else...something he didn't want to acknowledge, something that had been tormenting him for days.

Awareness...

Attraction...

Sex...

He swallowed hard, pushing back the feeling. He'd not experienced it before. Or at least, he hadn't allowed the thoughts to enter his head. But their relationship had changed, and Grant forced himself to admit one undisputable fact. Without knowing how, without even knowing what it meant, the truth was suddenly and glaringly obvious to him.

He was, without a doubt, hot for his wife. And that could mean only one thing.

Trouble.

Chapter Four

Of course Winona knew Grant would be at the ranch. It was his home, after all. But she'd promised her grandfather a visit and she would never intentionally let Red down. So, she gathered up her courage and walked across the yard and toward the corral.

There were a few cars parked out front of the main house and she recognized Joss's SUV. She waved a hand in Ellie's direction and barely spared him a glance. She was still mad at him for being such a jerk about the whole marriage situation. She didn't want him to be so in control—she wanted him to fall apart at the seams like she was. At least then she'd know he was *as* affected by what had transpired between them.

And she was annoyed that he looked so good, too. Why the hell couldn't he be a troll? She wished he didn't have a gaze so blisteringly intense she could barely meet his eyes. She wished they hadn't ruined everything by having sex. Even the marriage thing didn't seem so bad compared to the sex thing. Because having sex with Grant had definitely ruined everything.

"Hey," he said as she approached, and Winona managed a tight smile in his direction.

"Hi," she replied and stood beside Ellie, who was now hooking her arm around her elbow.

"Where've you been for the past couple of days?" Ellie asked.

Winona shrugged. "Just busy with work. Feel like going to Rusty's tonight? There's a good band playing."

Rusty's was a tavern in town—a little less formal than the O'Sullivan Hotel and not quite as family friendly as the Loose Moose. It was where the younger crowd hung out and a good place to have a couple of drinks and dance and unwind.

"Sounds like a great idea," Ellie said and looked toward her brother. "You in?"

His brows came up. "Am I invited?"

Ellie laughed and Winona ignored the dread settling in her belly. "Since you two are usually joined at the hip when you come home," Ellie said and jerked a thumb in both their directions. "I can't see why not."

Of course, her friend couldn't have known that her words would imply an intimacy that hadn't been there up until days ago, and when heat crawled up her neck at the idea of being joined to any part of Grant, Ellie gave her an odd look.

"Something wrong, Win?"

"Not a thing," Winona replied and shrugged. "I'm going to hang out with Papa for a while—catch you later," she said and untangled her arm, not looking at Grant as she walked off toward the cottages behind the main house.

Her grandfather's home wasn't the biggest of the four cottages, but he was incredibly house proud and had planted an amazing garden around the perimeter. She smiled when she saw he'd repainted the wishing well and the ornamental fairies placed around it. Situated beside a flowering arbor, it had always been one of her favorite spots to think and unwind when she was a child. She needed that thinking space more than ever at the moment. She was one step away from the porch when her grandfather opened the front door and greeted her, shuffling outside with the help of his walking stick, managing a lopsided grin.

"Hey, there's my favorite girl."

"Hi, Papa," she said and rushed up the steps to give him a hearty hug. He'd lost weight, she noticed, and frowned a little. "Have you been skipping dinner again?"

He tutted. "Now, don't be fussing around me. I eat

plenty. Mrs. B brings me a plate every evening and I've got plenty of treats in the freezer for snacks. I haven't heard from you for a few days," he said, slurring his words a bit, a sign that he probably hadn't been resting enough. "Everything okay?"

I got dumped by my fiancé, then married my best friend on a drunken rebound and slept with him!

"Everything's fine," she fibbed. "I thought we could do some gardening today," she suggested. "Last week you said you wanted some help planting in the vegetable patch."

"Nah," he said and grinned. "Ellie helped me out during the week."

Guilt pressed down on her shoulders. She'd been so busy screwing up her life in the past few days she'd neglected the one person who truly loved her. "Sorry."

"No need to be sorry," he said and waved a hand as they headed inside. "I know you're busy."

Her grandfather's cottage was neat and Winona felt immediately at ease the moment she crossed the threshold. They hung out for a while, chatting about Red's garden and the deck planking he'd planned on getting down now it was spring. She moved to the kitchen to get them both a drink and he asked about her job, and then, inevitably, about Dwight.

"Ah—well, actually," she said and poured lemonade, "Dwight and I broke up."

Her grandfather went silent for a moment, then

regarded her with his usual kind expression. "Well, can't say I'm surprised. I mean, you haven't seen each other for a while."

Winona swallowed the burn in her throat. As mad as she was with Dwight, and no matter how much his no-show at their wedding still hurt, she also felt a portion of relief. "I guess we both wanted different things," she said and shrugged. "It wasn't to be."

"Then I'm glad you broke it off," he said and sighed.

I didn't. He dumped me. Left me. Abandoned me.

"So," Winona said and quickly changed the subject, "what can I do to help around the place while I'm here?"

He made a few suggestions and they got busy cleaning and polishing the pieces inside the trophy cabinet. Most of them were from Red's early years as a bronc rider, but there was one shelf that stored Winona's scholastic accolades. Looking at the trophies, it seemed like such a long time ago—when she'd been filled with dreams of a real career. She'd always struggled with math, but once Grant took her under his wing and began tutoring her, she discovered a knack for numbers and imagined she'd have a career in the business sector. She didn't really know why she'd chosen to study history over business when she finally got to college. And she knew it was simply excuses that kept her from finishing her studies. She'd had the same conversation with

Grant many times over the years. Of course, he was always her staunchest supporter, but he didn't hold back his opinion, either. Like questioning her resistance to going into partnership with Regina at the bakery. It made sense. She could stay in Cedar River and be close to her grandfather, work with someone she liked and respected and sink her ambition into a thriving business. Yeah…it made complete sense to go for it.

But…

What if it didn't work out? What if the business failed and she lost everything she'd invested? Thinking about it made all her insecurities rush to the surface. Because logically, Winona knew it was fear holding her back.

Once they were done with the trophy cabinet it was lunchtime. She made sandwiches and poured apple cider and after they ate her grandfather went off for his daily nap. Winona hung around the cabin for ten minutes before finishing her drink and then heading outside. The sounds of the ranch were comforting and she made her way down the steps and walked around the house, and then toward the orchard.

She'd been sitting in a spot near the apple trees when she heard Grant approach and say her name. Winona turned and sighed, knowing her solitude was over.

He sat down beside her, stretched out his long

legs and crossed his arms. The aftershave he wore was as familiar to her as any scent on the ranch and she inhaled sharply, quickly evoking memories she knew she needed to forget. Skin, sweat, sighs, kisses that made her spin. *I shouldn't be remembering this.* But she did. So acutely it filled her with a kind of nervous energy.

"You know," he said, looking straight ahead, "you can't ignore me forever."

"I'm not ignoring you," she denied. "I'm spending time with my grandfather. At least, I was, but he's napping now. Did you want something?"

"Just to talk," he said easily. "Like we've *always* managed to do without complication for the last eighteen years."

The reminder made her throat ache. "Times change. Things change."

He uncrossed his arms and reached for her hand, holding it firmly within his own. "Winnie, we don't have to let this situation change anything."

She snorted. "Is that what we are? A *situation*?" she said and pulled her hand from his.

He let out a long sigh, clearly ignoring her question. "So…have you heard from the marine?"

Winona blinked. "No. And I don't expect to. He dumped me at the altar, remember?"

"I remember. Lucky escape, then?"

She laughed humorlessly. "Yeah…because things are so much better for me now."

"I'd never abandon you, Winnie, whatever the circumstances."

His words cut her through to the core. Of course she knew that. Grant would never make a promise and then not see it through because he possessed an innate integrity that defined him. Even with the women he dated, he was always honest about his intentions. Or rather, his *lack* of intentions.

"This must feel weird for you," she said and shrugged. "I mean, you've made it clear you never wanted to get married. I mean, not that we're really married…"

"Oh, we're *really* married," he corrected. "We've got the license to prove it. And everything else," he added and glanced her way.

Winona's skin heated as the memory returned. "Well, it wasn't that big a deal," she lied, recalling every blistering moment. "I think that's best forgotten, don't you?"

"I've never been good at pretending," he remarked and got to his feet. "And neither are you," he added and held out his hand. "Come on, Winnie, let's not worry about it for today and try and enjoy ourselves."

She hesitated, looking at his hand, thinking it was an olive branch of sorts, his way of keeping them connected and *normal*. But her fear was that they would never be normal again. Still, she took his hand, felt the warmth of his fingers linking with hers and a familiar sense of connection that, despite everything, forced her to admit that she needed him in her life. *Wanted* him in her life. Even when it seemed impossible. Or when she hurt deep down to her bones.

"So, you're going to see the lawyer on Monday?" she asked as they headed for the main house.

He nodded and gently swung their arms in a companionable way—much like they had done when they were kids. "That was the plan. Do you want to come?"

"I'm working Monday. But I have a break at one o'clock so I could meet you there if you can get an appointment for that time."

"Okay."

"It shouldn't be too complicated, should it?"

He shrugged a little as they headed for the back door and walked through the mudroom. "I don't think so. It's a no-contest divorce, so it should be simple enough."

The news should have cheered her up; instead, all she experienced was a deep-rooted wave of disappointment and unhappiness. Instead of being on a honeymoon, of sharing days and nights with her husband, of intimacy and soft whispers, of strong arms holding her, she was talking about divorce.

She pulled her hand from his as they entered the kitchen and were greeted by the sugary scent of baking and Mrs. Bailey's broad grin. The kitchen at the Triple C was the hub of the house, with its Shaker-style cabinets and long countertop, and she'd spent much of her childhood listening and learning recipes from the older woman.

"I wondered if I'd see you today," Mrs. B said and smiled, gesturing to a baking tray she was taking out of the oven. "I played around with that cookie recipe this week, you know, the one with the ginger pieces. I think they turned out much better with the secret ingredient."

Grant, who was very open about his cookie fetish, looked at them both. "What secret ingredient?"

Mrs. B chuckled. "Well, it wouldn't be a secret if we told you."

"Are you holding out on me, Mrs. B?" he teased and held a hand to his heart. "You know I'm addicted to your cooking."

She laughed again. "Enough with the charm. I remember the day you told me you were a vegetarian. I don't think your brothers believed you. You were, what, fourteen?"

"Fifteen," he replied. "So, about these cookies…"

Mrs. B continued to chuckle and placed the baking tray on the other side of the countertop, and away from Grant's swift hands. "I promised Joss he could have this batch."

Grant looked suitably affronted. "And here I was thinking I was your favorite?"

"Of course you are," the older woman replied and quickly passed him a cookie. "Now, off you go, the pair of you."

He devoured the cookie in two bites and then Winona ushered them from the kitchen. It felt nice to laugh, she thought as they headed up the hallway and toward the living room. Joss's daughters, almost thirteen-year-old Sissy and ten-year-old Clare, were sitting on the sofa, an electronic tablet in hand and earbuds in their ears. Joss had lost his wife eight years earlier and had raised his girls as a single dad ever since. They had always treated Winona as an honorary and much-loved aunt, and she relished the role. Joss and Mitch were also in the room, and Winona made her way toward the girls while Grant hung out with his brothers. She loved spending time with the girls and they were quick to show her their latest downloaded movies on their tablets. She'd been their babysitter countless times over the years and always helped out Joss when she could. Family was like that, she thought, and now more than ever she felt as though she needed them. Perhaps she could reach out to Ellie, or Mitch's wife, Tess. She was sure either woman would understand her predicament and offer consolation and sensible advice.

And yet…she didn't want to overstep. She didn't want to assume anything.

They were Grant's family. Not hers. She had her grandfather. And since she wasn't about to burden Red with her troubles, Winona knew one thing.

She was alone.

Grant watched Winnie and couldn't ignore the heat churning in his belly. Things were so tense between them and he didn't know how to fix it. Strange for him, because fixing things was what he did. Well, in his work at least. He'd always figured he was missing the gene that his brothers had—the one where they made getting close to people look seamless. At least, that's how nearly all of his siblings made it look. Well, all of them except for Jake. But even his second oldest brother had embraced family, fatherhood and responsibility since returning to town nearly two years ago. Sure, Grant loved his siblings, but deep down he believed that losing his parents when he was young had switched off something inside him. He wasn't sure how to define it, how to explain the sense of disconnect he experienced whenever Mitch, Jake or Joss talked about being married, or being a father.

It made him think about Billie-Jack and for a moment he was tempted to spill to his brothers that the old man had reached out. In his heart, he knew exactly how his siblings would react. *If* he decided to meet with his father, Grant knew he had to do it alone—at least at first.

He caught Winnie's gaze, and when she raised a brow he realized he was frowning. Of course, she knew his moods better than anyone. But it went both ways. She was unhappy and Grant knew he was partly responsible for the way she was feeling. He left his brothers and walked across the room to where she sat with his nieces and plonked in the chair opposite.

"What?" she demanded sharply.

"Nothing," he replied and stretched out his legs. "Just hanging out with my favorite girls."

Sissy and Clare chuckled and quickly bombarded him with computer questions, perching on either side of the chair. They stayed like that for a while, until his brothers left the room in search of snacks, with Joss quickly calling his daughters to the kitchen as they left.

Grant rested his elbows on the chair arms and looked at Winnie. "So, I was thinking about what Regina said this morning."

Her gaze narrowed. "You were?"

He nodded. "Well, yeah—I was thinking that if you're interested in taking on the bakery and you need funds, I could—"

"What? Be my financial backer?"

"Why not?" he said, shifting in the chair. "Wouldn't you do it for me if the situation was reversed?"

She sat farther back. "Well…yeah…but this isn't the same—"

"Of course it's the same," he said, cutting her off. "And for the record, we've been having this same conversation for the past twelve months. But if you're so hell-bent on doing things by yourself, we could make it official and draw it up like a proper loan with interest and a payment plan. Don't let your pride stand in the way of getting what you want."

"No."

Grant sighed. "I don't understand you, Winnie."

"Understand what?" she shot back and sprang forward in the seat. "That I want to make my way in the world on my own terms, without taking handouts from friends or family? You did it—why is it so hard to comprehend that I want to do the same?"

"If you remember, Mitch paid for my college tuition," he reminded her.

"That was different," she said and exhaled heavily. "The Triple C is as much your legacy as your siblings' and Mitch is your brother."

"And you're my best friend," he said flatly. "Plus, I might add, my wife."

She shushed him quickly, looking around to make sure no one else heard his words. "Technically, not literally."

Grant smiled a little. "You don't think? So, how long do two people have to know one another and how much sex do they have to have before they are *literally* married?"

He saw color rise up her neck. "Can you *not* joke? This isn't funny."

His smile increased. "I'm just trying to lighten the mood, Winnie. But I'm right, though, about the bakery. Unless you want to work at the tourist center forever?"

"Of course I don't, but it's a job. Besides, since when have you been such a job snob?"

"I'm not," he replied. "If working at the tourist center satisfied you and it was the job of your dreams, I'd support you one hundred percent. But I've seen you baking here with Mrs. B and I know how happy it makes you. Plus, you're much more savvy when it comes to numbers and retail than you realize." He sighed. "Look, just promise me you'll at least think about it."

She stopped scowling and tossed her hair in a way that struck him as sexy. Had she always done that? He'd never noticed before. But something about the action hitched up his awareness a notch or two.

"Okay, I'll think about it," she said and then excused herself, leaving the room quickly, the scent of her fragrance lingering in the air.

Once he was alone, Grant tried to compartmentalize his feelings. True, he'd always known Winnie was beautiful. But something had changed, like there had been a cosmic shift in his thinking. There was something in the way she spoke, the way she moved, that brought other feelings to the surface. Like a slowly building desire that amplified every time he looked at her. There was memory, too—of holding her and touching her and having her in his arms. It was a shock, thinking about her in any other way than as his best friend. He figured he should feel as guilty as hell, but oddly he didn't.

It will pass...

He said the words to himself a couple of times, trying to clear his head, to forget the memory and get on with the present. He had a job in San Francisco coming up, for a large hotel that had recently switched management software and were having all kinds of tech problems. Grant had worked on a couple of hotels in the past and expected to be gone for at least a week. Maybe the time away would be good for his relationship with Winnie. She'd have a chance to think about his offer to help her invest in the bakery and get accustomed to their impending divorce.

Thinking he had it all figured out, Grant got to his feet and joined his brothers and nieces in the kitchen. Winnie wasn't there and he figured she'd returned to her grandfather's cabin. Ellie was sitting at the counter beside Tess, and Mitch was also there, holding his young son, Charlie. He tapped his oldest brother's shoulder affectionately. The truth was, even though there was little more than six years between them, Mitch was more like a father than their own had ever been. He both loved and respected his brother and owed him a debt of gratitude for keeping him on the straight and narrow during his school years. It had been hard at first, and Grant had rebelled, skipping classes, missing assignments—but by the time he hit sophomore year, Grant pulled himself together and took his studies seriously, making plans for a future career in software engineering. Now he got paid a lot of money to do something he loved, and he knew Mitch had played a huge part in his success.

He watched his family interact and again thought

about Billie-Jack's sudden resurfacing. Mitch, he knew, would calmly warn him away from making the connection. Jake would probably tell him to say go straight to hell. And Hank—who had more reason to hate Billie-Jack than any of them—would advise him to do what he felt was right. He figured he should start with Joss, who always said what was on his mind, and could always be relied upon for a dose of honesty.

Grant hung around the house for the remainder of the afternoon and it was past six o'clock when Ellie reminded him that they were heading to Rusty's. Joss had dropped his girls off at his in-laws' that afternoon and said he'd meet them there. He knew Winnie had left the ranch around four and figured she was also hooking up with them at Rusty's. Or maybe not. Perhaps hanging out with him was the last thing she wanted to do?

He and Ellie headed into town and pulled up outside Rusty's around seven that evening. There were a few cars out front and he recognized Joss's tow truck in the parking area. He pulled up beside the truck and Ellie was quick to get out. Grant glanced around for Winona's car and when he realized it wasn't there his gut dropped.

"Did you say something?" Ellie asked when she came around his car.

Grant shook his head. "No."

They headed inside and Ellie waved to Joss the moment they spotted his brother by the bar ordering drinks and chatting up the pretty bartender. Grant was following Ellie toward one of the booth seats when he spotted a woman in jeans, boots and a bright colored halter top, with long dark hair. She was standing by the small stage, laughing and talking to one of the band members. Winnie. She looked incredible. For a moment he felt as though his heart had stopped beating. It didn't make sense. He'd seen her dressed up countless times. Sex had messed up his brain—there was no other explanation. The band began playing and she quickly joined them at the booth, sliding across the seat opposite him.

"I didn't see your car outside," Grant remarked.

She shrugged lightly. "I came with Regina. Her boyfriend is the drummer."

Grant vaguely remembered and his gut relaxed a little when he realized that was why she looked to be so friendly with the band.

"The bass player is cute," Ellie said and grinned as Joss joined them with a round of drinks.

She shrugged again. "He's okay."

"Does your boyfriend know you have a thing for bass players, Win?" Joss teased and sat down beside her.

"Dwight and I broke up," Winnie said flatly, not looking at anyone.

"What?" Ellie squealed. "When did this happen?"

"A couple of days ago," she replied and briefly met Grant's gaze.

Ellie grabbed a drink. "What happened?"

Winnie shrugged. "Oh, you know, long-distance relationships never work out."

"That's true," Joss said agreeably and winked. "So, the bass player?"

"I don't think so," she replied. "I'm not in the market for a rebound relationship just yet."

Ouch.

Grant felt the sting of her words and shifted in his seat. He drank some beer and listened to his sister prattle out more questions as the band changed songs, doing a slow cover of a Creedence classic.

"So, who broke up with who?" Ellie asked. "Is he seeing someone else? Do you think he was cheating on you and that's why he—"

"Winnie," Grant said when he saw her pinched expression. "You love this song—let's dance."

She looked startled for a second and then quickly agreed, shimmying out of the booth and heading for the dance floor. Grant met her in the middle of several other couples and grasped her hand. They'd danced before—at weddings, at Rusty's, even in her small apartment above the bakery when she tried to teach him how to rumba. But he experienced an odd sensation rippling through his limbs as they moved closer together. Her fingers curled around his shoulders and he rested his hands around her waist, settling on her hips.

"Thanks," she said, speaking closely into his ear. "I wasn't in the mood for an inquisition."

"I figured," he said, ignoring the way his knee brushed between her thighs. "I know Ellie can be relentless when she wants intel."

She relaxed a little. "People will be curious, I guess."

"How did Red take the news about the marine?"

"Oh, you know Papa—he was cool about it. Probably relieved, although he would never say so."

"Well, he undoubtedly thinks no one is good enough for his little girl," Grant said and grinned. "Maybe he's right."

"Oh, I don't know," she said and swayed. "He's a fan of yours, so would probably welcome our, you know, *situation* with open arms."

Grant heard the tremor in her voice and felt every ounce of the obviously mixed emotions in her heart. It pained him. He never wanted to see Winnie hurting.

"We'll work it out," he assured her. "I promise."

She nodded, resting her head against his shoulder. "I hope so."

It felt good to have her so close. Like they were still as connected—as tightly bound together in friendship—as always. And he liked the way she felt in his arms. Her perfume, some floral scent he would recognize blindfolded, swirled around them and the familiarity of it strangely settled his frayed nerves.

"We'll see the lawyer Monday and by the time I get back from San Francisco it will be well on the way to being finalized."

"Oh, that's right, you're leaving soon," she said and sighed.

"Wednesday," he confirmed. "But I'll call you while I'm away. As usual."

But he knew she wasn't convinced. There was nothing *usual* about what was hanging between them.

And they both knew it.

Chapter Five

They had an appointment to see the lawyer at 1:15 p.m. on Monday afternoon and Winona greeted Grant outside Tyler Madden's office right on time. She'd met Tyler a few times and had always found him to be polite and professional. He didn't offer any opinion about their situation other than give them quick and concise advice on the steps they were required to take towards dissolving their marriage.

She sat quietly beside Grant, noticing how tight his shoulders were as they listened to the lawyer and when Tyler asked the obvious question.

"And you're sure this is what you both want?"

"Absolutely," Grant replied.

Winona's insides contracted at the swiftness of

his reply and then she got mad at herself for being so ridiculous. Of course, divorce was what they both wanted. There was no other option.

"Yes," she said. "Of course."

When the meeting was over, she felt oddly drained, like she needed to sleep, or at least to shut her eyes for a while and not think about the chaos that had suddenly become her life.

Once they were finished at Tyler's office, she quickly said she had somewhere else to be.

"Do you feel like getting coffee?" he asked. "Or maybe—"

"No, sorry, I gotta go."

"Sure," he said, clearly aware of her need to rush away. "Ah…so I'll call you while I'm out of town," he reminded her.

Winona *did* want to get away—from him, from *them*, from the ache that had suddenly lodged in her chest. "Yeah…whatever."

Then she bailed, hightailing it along the sidewalk as fast as she could without looking like she was running. And knowing that he'd remained where he was, watching her as she disappeared from view.

But true to his word, Grant called her while he was in San Francisco. Not every night, but enough to maintain a connection. That didn't mean Winona actually looked forward to his calls. Because it wasn't like before.

Before Vegas.

Before her world had turned upside down.

He was annoyingly upbeat about everything when he spoke, and Winona tried to be the same. She tried ignoring the word *divorce* and didn't think about the time they were together, dancing at Rusty's, pretending as though everything was normal between them. Instead, she pretended that he was on any other work trip and it was any other moment in time. But it wasn't. Because the tension between them was undeniable.

In the meantime, as the week ended and another week dragged along, Winona had decided she needed to make some serious life changes. A new career—or a career, full stop—was definitely a priority. Making a decision about the bakery. Talking to the bank and her accountant. Perhaps even getting a bigger apartment or even a house once she was more financially settled. And yeah, maybe a dog or a cat. Finding some new friends.

Yes, she needed to make plans and see them through.

And would have done exactly that if not for one tiny wrench in her works.

One huge wrench actually.

Her period was late.

Four days late. And she was *never* late.

Which was why she was sitting on the edge of the bathtub in her bathroom, staring at the pregnancy test she'd taken thirty seconds earlier. Waiting. The longest five-minute wait of her life.

By the second minute, she'd convinced herself

that her late period was simply a reaction to stress and she had nothing to worry about. By the third minute, she began to worry. By the fourth minute, she was on the verge of a panic attack. When her phone's alarm pinged at the five-minute mark, Winona snatched up the test and stared at the results.

Two lines.

Positive.

Pregnant.

Oh, my God!

She sucked in a few quick breaths and clutched the edge of the bathtub.

Could it be real?

She looked at the test again. She was really pregnant. A baby. Motherhood. Life-will-never-be-the-same-again. Her brain felt like it was going to seriously overheat, and she took another succession of breaths, desperate to calm her pulse. She had to think clearly.

This can't be happening...

But she knew it was. In her heart, she'd known it for days. From the first day her period was late. Because she was never late. And now, unlike never before, she was paying the price for her foolishness. Which included her quick decision to accept the marriage proposal of a man she'd barely spent any time with since they started dating, and then rushing off to Vegas with some silly notion of the whole thing being romantic. As though Dwight was the great love of her life. When she knew he wasn't, even before she'd agreed to marry him. It wasn't love that drew her to Dwight. It was her need to be loved. To be wanted. To be a part of someone's life. Her behavior was foolish and impulsive. Grant was right. She should never have done it.

Grant! God, how was he going to react?

She stared at the results again and shuddered, turning cold all over.

Her life was now irrevocably changed. And so was his.

Winona got to her feet, still clutching the pregnancy test, and headed for the kitchen on the shakiest knees she'd ever experienced. She tucked the test in her pocket, washed her hands and made tea. Decaf, she figured, and rummaged in the cupboard for the right tea bags. She found them, made tea and sat on the sofa by the window, staring out at the darkening street.

It was Monday evening and she'd worked for most of the day, the uneasiness growing within her each hour when she thought about the test she'd discreetly purchased at Talbot's drugstore during her lunch break. The tourist center had had a busy day, with several busloads of travelers coming in to pick up brochures about local events and Black Hills memorabilia. By the time she was home she was exhausted. And now, looking out across Main Street, watching the solitary set of traffic lights change every few minutes, seeing commuters driving home, or stopping outside JoJo's for pizza pickup, that somehow amplified her exhaustion and loneliness. Normally, she'd just call Grant, explain she was feeling *blah*, and they'd talk for a while. But she couldn't call him without *telling* him, and she simply wasn't ready to face it.

She wasn't sure how long she sat like that, just staring out at the street, but when her cell rang after eight, she quickly glanced at the number, saw that it was Grant and let it go to voice mail. She waited ten minutes before listening to the message.

"Hey, it's me. Just checking to make sure you're okay. I'm wrapped up here and will be home tomorrow. My boss has given me a few days off, so I'll call you when I'm in town. We really need to talk. I miss you."

Winona listened to the message again. And then again. It was similar to other messages she'd received in the past week and she shouldn't read any more into his words. He couldn't possibly know anything was wrong. So, he wanted to talk. Probably about their impending divorce. She responded with a thumbs-up emoji and headed for the shower, determined to get thoughts of him out of her head for a while.

When she returned to the living room she grabbed her laptop and starting searching for information about the early stages of pregnancy. Since she was just over two weeks along, she wanted to ensure she was prepared for what was to come. However, she knew one thing—Winona had every intention of having her baby. Of course, she knew it wouldn't be easy and had never anticipated she'd be a single mom. But she didn't care. Now that the initial shock had subsided, she was thinking clearer with each passing moment. She was facing the ultimate responsibility and now, more than ever, needed to make some significant changes to her life.

Firstly, though, she needed to tell Grant.

And she knew, without a doubt, that he would freak out at the news.

He didn't want to be a father. He'd made his feelings about marriage and fatherhood clear to her many times over the years. He wasn't interested in commitment. She knew his feelings were wrapped up in what had happened with Billie-Jack and she supposed she couldn't blame him. She had her own abandonment issues, after all.

So, she'd tell him and he could make up his own mind about what level of involvement he wanted. Plenty of people juggled parenthood without being in a real relationship.

She went to bed with a semiclear head, knowing she had decisions to make. When she got up it was past seven. She had a short shift that day and didn't start until eleven, so she cleaned up a little around the apartment, spent an hour or so looking at Instagram pictures of nursery rooms, made an appointment to see her local GP and then headed to work after she had a late breakfast.

The afternoon dragged on, though, and she was pleased when her shift ended. She dropped by the supermarket to pick up a few much needed groceries and got home around six o'clock to find Grant standing by his car, which he'd parked outside the bakery. He wore work clothes and she wondered if he'd come directly from the airport.

"Hey," he said as she approached and quickly took the grocery bags from her.

"You're back?"

He nodded. "I said I would be."

She looked him over. "Did you come straight from the airport?"

"Yes. I was hoping you'd be free for dinner. Feel like pizza?"

"Sure."

He followed her up the stairs, and once they were inside she unpacked the groceries while he called JoJo's and ordered their dinner. Winona busied herself in the kitchen while he left to collect the pizza, and when he returned she had the table set and two sodas opened.

He dropped the pizza box on the table. "Are you okay?" he asked, his expression narrow and concerned.

"Fine," she replied as she sat. "How was the trip?"

"Long," he said and slid into the seat opposite. "Ten days in a hotel room is way too many."

Winona nodded agreeably and served out the pizza, picking the extra peppers off her piece and adding them to his slice. "You look tired."

He exhaled heavily. "I feel tired. What about you, what have you been up to?"

Winona caught the breath in her throat and the truth teetered. The longer she put it off, the harder it would be. "So, you said in your message last night that you wanted to talk?"

He nodded. "Yeah…ah…the lawyer has the papers ready. I managed to get an appointment at nine tomorrow morning, so if that works for you we can sign them and get them filed in the court."

Winona's belly sank. She didn't know why. She'd been expecting it. She wanted it.

"Sure, no problem. I'm not working until eleven tomorrow morning."

He nodded again and she noticed his tightly drawn expression. She knew him too well to put it down to simple fatigue. He was tense and conflicted—just as she was. She thought about the baby growing inside and wondered, as she'd been doing all day, who he or she would look like. Would their child inherit Grant's green eyes, or would he or she be darker, with black hair and brown eyes? Would their child grow up to be calm and controlled, like he was, or quick-tempered and reactive? Would their child have horses and ranching in their blood?

Winona knew so little about her own father and wondered if she'd made a mistake by not pushing her mother for details when they spoke. Communication with her mom was so rare and sporadic she figured there was little point in dredging up the past, but now that she was having a child of her own, she did have a deeper curiosity.

"What are you thinking about?" he asked, picking up on her faraway look.

"My father," she said before she had a chance to snatch the words back. "I was just wondering, you know, what he was like. Or if I should try and ask my mother about him again."

He shrugged lightly. "You could. Do you think she'll tell you any more than you already know?"

"I'm not sure, but the older I get, the more curious I get. Then again, if I did find him and he rejected me…" Her words trailed off painfully. "I don't think I could bear that."

"We both got screwed over in the father department."

There was a coldness in his voice she hadn't heard for a long time. When they were kids, she knew how much his father's departure had wounded him. Over the years he seemed to have found peace with it. But maybe not. She watched him, felt the tension emanating from the stillness in his jaw and tight, unmoving shoulders.

"At least you knew your dad," she offered and drank a little soda. "That's something."

"He was an abusive drunk," Grant said, eyes down, not seeming to focus on anything in particular.

"Perhaps he's changed."

He looked up sharply, meeting her gaze. "He left us, Winnie. There's no coming back from that."

"I guess the trick is to break the cycle," she said,

almost holding her breath. "You know, being a better parent than the ones we've got."

His shoulders relaxed fractionally. "Well, my brothers seem to be doing a better job." He sighed, dropped the pizza slice in his hand and stared at her. "Sorry to be such a killjoy."

She managed a gentle smile. "You don't seem like yourself."

"I've got things on my mind."

He wasn't the only one...

She took a breath, spotting an opening even though she'd had no intention of announcing anything over dinner. But there was no time like the present. And he needed to know the truth. "Well, actually, there's something I need to—"

"Billie-Jack called me," he said flatly, cutting her off, his words almost freezing the air between them.

Winona reeled back. She knew Grant's feelings for his father were conflicted—she also knew he was aware of the fact. It was a complicated situation for the whole family. "What? When?"

"He's left a couple of messages in the last month," he replied. "He wants to reconnect."

Winona swallowed hard. "What are you going to do?"

He shrugged tightly. "I have no idea."

"Have you told your brothers or Ellie?" she asked.

"Nope."

Winona looked at him, saw the tension tightening his shoulders and knew that it wasn't the right moment to tell him about the baby. For one, he looked beat, and it wasn't the kind of news he needed to hear when he was tired, mentally exhausted and clearly had so much else on his mind.

"Do you think he wants money? Or something else?" she asked quietly.

"I'm not sure what he wants. I haven't seen him for eighteen years," he said and ran a weary hand through his hair. "Can I crash here tonight? I don't feel like being at the ranch when I'm in this mood. Or driving home."

It smacked of familiarity. A familiarity she wasn't sure was such a great idea. But of course she would never turn him away. He was her friend. *My husband. The father of my child.* As she thought the words, a heavy ache weighed down on her chest, but she managed a tight smile.

"Sure," she said and motioned to the couch. "It's all yours."

They finished up the pizza, drank the soda and managed to get through the following hour with very little conversation. He headed downstairs to grab his bag and was back a few minutes later.

"Okay if I take a shower?" he asked.

Winona finished clearing the plates and nodded. Once he was out of sight and she heard the water hissing, she relaxed a little. It had never been like this between them. Usually, she could deal with him being in her apartment, in her bathroom, in her life. He'd bunked over countless times. But so much had changed between them and she couldn't quite compartmentalize her feelings.

When he returned, he wore low-slung jeans, a white T-shirt that clung to his chest and loafers. He looked much more relaxed, though, and she managed a tight smile in his direction.

"Better?" she queried.

"Much," he said and rounded out his shoulders as he moved into the kitchen to stand beside her. "Thanks again."

"No worries," she replied. "Would you like coffee? Or tea? I have beer in the fridge."

"No, I'm good. If it's okay I might chill out on the sofa for a while and watch a little TV to try and clear my head before bed."

Winona glanced at the clock on the wall. "Of course. I'm going to take a shower and go to bed. See you in the morning."

"Sure," he said and grasped her hand, rubbing his thumb over hers for a moment. "Winnie, once we get through this, everything will get back to normal. I promise."

Winona drew in a long breath and pulled her hand from his, then reached up and touched his face. His eyes were brilliantly green and regarded her with burning intensity. She stayed like that for a moment, connected to him, feeling the pulse in his jaw beneath her thumb.

"The thing is, Grant," she said and dropped her

hand, "you can't make me that promise. Not now. Not ever again."

Then she walked off, her heart so heavy in her chest she actually ached.

Grant woke up the following morning with a crick in his neck and pain in his hip. He stretched out on the sofa, groaned and swung his feet onto the floor. He checked his phone, saw that it was 7:20 and stood. Looks like he *wasn't* going for his predictable 6:15 run. The apartment was quiet and he figured Winona was still asleep, so he headed for the kitchen and was filling the coffee filter when the front door opened and she came into the apartment carrying take-out coffee cups and a brown bag.

"I bought breakfast," she announced and then made a face as she placed them on the countertop. "Well, actually, Regina didn't charge me this morning. I *have* breakfast," she corrected. "How did you sleep?"

"Lousy," he replied and rubbed the back of his neck. "I prefer a bed to a couch."

She looked at him oddly, and he wondered if she found his statement provocative. He hadn't mean it to sound that way. The truth was, he was tired of trying to make everything sound normal between them.

"Pecan Danish for me, and some kind of vegan-friendly muffin for you," she said after a moment.

Grant grabbed his coffee and muffin and walked to the small dining table. "Thanks."

She remained by the counter, watching him, and he felt her scrutiny down to the soles of his feet. "We'll head to the lawyer's office and pick up those papers first thing," he said and sipped his coffee.

She nodded and moved to the table, taking a seat opposite, placing her cup in front of her.

Then she took a breath, as deep as he'd ever heard. "I have to tell you something."

Grant's gaze narrowed. She looked pale, he noticed, and out of sorts. Had she been like that last night? Had he been too wrapped up in his own thoughts he hadn't realized? He recalled their phone conversations over the last week or so and realized they'd spoken about very little. Concern burrowed deep and he tried to lighten his expression. "What is it?"

"It's important. Really important."

"Okay," he said, uneasiness pooling in his gut. "Go ahead, I'm listening."

"Well, I'm...the thing is... I'm..." Her words trailed off and she sighed heavily. "Oh, hell, there's no easy way to say this."

She reached into her jeans and pulled something from the pocket, then slid it across the table. It was about five inches long and white, and the moment he registered what it was, Grant's stomach plummeted. He stared at it, then looked at Winnie, and then again at the damning piece of plastic. He'd never seen one up close, of course. He'd never been in that situation. But still, he knew exactly what it was.

"That's a pregnancy test," he said and swallowed hard, white noise suddenly screeching between his ears.

"Yes, it is."

He took a breath, as deep as he could, trying to get some air into his lungs. "Is it positive?"

She nodded. "Yes."

"You're pregnant?"

Grant couldn't believe the hollow voice asking the question was his. But he was in shock, the kind of shock that started at the feet and worked its way up, polarizing movement. His chest tightened and for a fleeting moment it was impossible to breathe and he wondered if he was going to pass out.

"Yes, I am," she replied quietly.

Grant met her gaze. "I don't... I can't... It's not..." He stopped speaking before he said something stupid and got to his feet, pacing the room, hands on hips, head spinning. *Pregnant.* He inhaled and turned to face her, registering what it actually meant. "It's mine?"

She nodded again. "Yes."

"You're sure?"

Her beautiful mouth thinned. "Am I sure I'm pregnant, or am I sure that it's yours?"

He quickly realized how bad the question sounded. "I didn't mean to—"

"What?" she shot back, her voice so quiet he knew she was annoyed. "Accuse me of lying? Question my integrity?"

"Of course not," he said raggedly. "I'm just…you know…in shock."

"The baby is yours, Grant," she said flatly. "My boyfriend was deployed overseas, remember? Then he dumped me at the altar. Then we got drunk, got married and had sex—you recall all that happening, right?"

"I…we used birth control," he said, the memory rushing in and out. "At least, I think we did."

She shrugged. "Well, it mustn't have worked, because I don't sleep around."

Grant finally managed to take a breath, dropped into the love seat by the window and swore softly. Of course he knew that about her. "Sorry. I'm kind of reeling here… I can't quite believe it."

She pushed back her shoulders. "That's how I felt when I found out the other day. Today, I see things a lot clearer."

"You do?"

She nodded. "I'm going to have this baby, Grant… if that's the next question you intend on asking me."

He wasn't sure what he was going to say. A baby? Winnie was having his baby. It seemed too surreal to believe. "Like I said, I'm in shock. So, do you feel okay? Not sick or anything?"

"No," she replied. "I feel fine. I made an appointment to see my GP on Monday. I'm a couple of weeks along, so it's too early for an ultrasound. But I'll let you know when I get one—I mean, if you're interested."

Grant stared at her, more confused than he had ever been in his life. Interested? What did that mean? She doubted him? She wondered what he'd do? Or wouldn't do? "Do you think I won't step up?"

She shrugged. "I don't know what to think about you anymore. Let's face it, the last couple of weeks haven't exactly been business as usual for us, have they? The truth is, all I've really thought about for the past couple of days is the baby I'm carrying. And you're right, it's a shock, but I'm not going to lie and say I'm *unhappy* about it. Scared out of my mind, yes. Terrified I'm going to screw it up, absolutely. But, Grant, you have to make up your own mind about how you feel about it," she said levelly. "I can't tell you how to feel. I can't make you react a certain way. I can't force you to be a father to this child. Step up, or don't, it's completely up to you."

The conviction in her voice was resolute and unwavering. He knew that about her. Knew that she could be stubborn and hard-nosed about things. Like not borrowing money to invest in the bakery. Like eloping with the marine. She would do it without him—that was very clear.

"We have to go," he said, suddenly impatient to clear his head and take some time to think about what she'd told him. "We have an appointment with the lawyer, remember?"

"I remember," she said flatly. "And don't forget to take your stuff with you when we leave. If you're going to be staying in town for a few days, we can sign the divorce papers right away. I think we both know that the quicker we fix this, the better."

He nodded, barely able to draw in breath, and then quickly changed his clothes. They left her apartment shortly after, without speaking more than half a dozen words to one another, and dumped his bag in the car before they walked to the lawyer's office, two blocks away. Even though Winnie was at his side and he could feel the tension vibrating through her, the walk did him some good and managed to clear his head a little.

A baby?

He'd never thought about fatherhood much in relation to himself—only in an abstract kind of way. Since he wasn't convinced he was a marriage-and-white-picket-fence kind of guy, the idea of being a parent rarely crossed his thoughts. No doubt his resistance had something to do with his own screwed-up relationship with Billie-Jack.

A baby with Winnie?

That was the killer. Of all the turns he might have expected their relationship to take, having a kid together had never been on the radar. Losing her to the marine—well, yeah—of course he'd thought about that possibility. Being friends for life? Yes, he'd thought that, too. He'd even thought she'd have kids one day and maybe make him their godfather. But having a baby together, that was bigger than big.

He remembered their night together in Vegas, and then was quickly pleading with his brain to switch off the images suddenly bombarding his thoughts. Skin, heat, sweat, kissing and touching, pleasure on a cosmic scale. He knew it was foolish and irresponsible behavior. He knew he should have pulled on every ounce of his self-control that night and ignored the way his body reacted to her. He shouldn't have kissed her when she'd asked him to. He shouldn't have stroked her skin and gotten lost in her touch. He should have shown strength. And hell, the *character* he'd always considered made him the man he was.

But he hadn't. He'd shown weakness. She'd kissed his neck, touched his chest, pressed herself against him, and he was quickly reverted to putty. Sure, they were drunk and that had clearly impaired their senses. But somewhere during that night reality *should* have checked in. He should have been able to drag himself away from her—no matter how much it would have cost. Because even though he knew she would have felt rejected and alone, that risk should have outweighed everything else.

And now they had a baby coming.

It was mind-blowing and too much to think about. They were two doors away from their destination when he spotted his brother Joss coming out of the drugstore. He wasn't in the mood for family just yet. Telling anyone seemed irresponsible. And the way Winnie dug him in the ribs with her elbow made it clear she felt exactly the same way.

"Hey, you two," Joss said as he greeted them and

quickly looked toward Grant. "I didn't know you were in town. What's going on?"

Grant's clear head quickly disappeared and suddenly he felt like he was on the verge of a full-blown panic attack. "Ah—just taking a few days off. What about you?"

His brother held up a small brown bag. "Clare's asthma medication. Being a dad is a 24/7 job," Joss said and grinned. "But I love it."

Grant's insides crumbled. How could he possibly match being father of the year like his brother? Joss had the parenting gene ingrained in his DNA, like Mitch. Grant didn't even own a cat. He had friends. A job he enjoyed. He dated when he felt like it. Nothing serious. There was nothing *edgy* about his life. But in that moment, he felt like he was about to fall off a cliff.

"Are you okay?" Joss asked with a frown. "You look like crap."

He heard Winnie suck in a breath and hated that his brother could work out his moods so easily. Grant quickly shook some life into his limbs. "I'm fine," he lied. "Just tired. I gotta go, errands to run, but I'll catch up with you and the girls while I'm in town." He shook his brother's hand and waited for a second while Winnie gave Joss a brotherly hug and then they headed down the street, not looking back, and hoping that Joss didn't notice they took a left turn and walked into Tyler Madden's law practice.

"That was close," she breathed once they were in the small waiting room.

"Yeah," he replied. Too close. He loathed sneaking around. With Billie-Jack resurfacing and the situation with Winnie, Grant felt as though he was being suffocated by secrets.

Ten minutes later, after a short consult, Tyler gave them the documents they needed to sign. "So, that's it?"

Tyler nodded. "Yes. It's a fairly straightforward process. It's a no-contest divorce and there are no assets to divide and no children."

Grant was sure his heart stopped beating. He looked at Winnie, pale and rigid in the chair beside him, her back so straight it looked as though it might snap. "If there were kids…things would be different?"

The other man nodded again. "Of course. Children change everything. Once you've both signed the forms, bring them back and I'll file them in court. About sixty days after that, the marriage will be over."

Over…

Children change everything…

They left the office shortly after, the envelope in his hand.

"You sign it first," she said, her hands clutched together. "Drop them off when you're done."

"Winnie, I—"

"Let's just fix this, okay?" she said quietly. "I have to get ready for work. I'll talk to you…whenever."

She walked off, her shoulders so tight he knew she was barely hanging on. But she would, that was her way. There was a resilience to Winnie, a strength she possessed that never failed to amaze him, even now.

Grant headed to his car. He knew Winnie didn't finish work until three so he had a few hours to fill before they could talk again—something he knew they needed to do. Instead of heading out to the ranch he stayed in town, driving around, buying coffee and sitting in the park for a while, answering emails on his phone, thinking about anything and everything except the reality staring him in the face.

His future.

His child.

His wife.

He got back to her apartment at 3:25 that afternoon and tapped on the door. He had a key, but it seemed oddly invasive letting himself in. She answered the door quickly and he was struck by how beautiful she looked. Her hair was down, flowing over her shoulders, and her wide brown eyes seemed huge in her face.

"We really need to talk," he said quietly.

She stared at him. "Tomorrow."

"This can't wait," he said and strode past her. Once he was in the apartment, Grant turned to face her, holding out the envelope. "I don't want to sign the divorce papers."

She gasped. "What?"

"We can't get divorced, Winnie," he said, hearing his own voice like it belonged to someone else. But still, he knew it had to be said. "Not now. We have to stay married."

Chapter Six

Winona stared at Grant in disbelief. He'd clearly lost his mind and was making zero sense.

"Stay married?" she echoed incredulously. "What? Why?"

"Because of the baby," he replied and exhaled. "Why else."

Winona drew in a shuddering breath. "You can't be serious?"

"Perfectly," he said. "I think our child should be born to parents who are married, don't you?"

Of course divorce wasn't ideal. But neither was staying married for the sake of the baby. "I don't think that matters much these days."

"It matters to me," he said. "And since we're married anyway, what difference will it make? It's not like we have to plan a wedding or do anything."

She took a moment to digest his words and then sat down. "So, you're saying we should *stay* married, not that we should *be* married, correct?"

He scowled. "What's the difference?"

"Night and day," she replied, ignoring the heat filling her blood. "If we stay married, we just go about our business as usual. If we *are* married— that's a whole different ball game."

"I don't see how."

She huffed a breath. "Because it means living together, *being* together, sleeping in the same bed, arguing over who gets the remote. You know, marriage."

He quickly looked like he'd been smacked in the face with a truth stick. "Well, yeah, but I think—"

"No buts," she said, her hand instinctively settling on her belly. "You don't really want to be married to me, right?"

"I want to do the right thing," he replied earnestly.

Winona didn't know if she wanted to hug him or hit him. But she knew that about Grant; she knew he oozed integrity and had probably spent the last few hours considering his options and coming up with one clear winner—that a baby meant they should stay in their marriage. But Winona wasn't so black and white. She might not be the most world-wise woman on the planet, but she knew a potential disaster when she saw one.

"You can be a father," she assured him, "without being a husband."

His expression blanched. "You mean part-time?"

"Plenty of men do it," she replied.

"Doesn't mean I want to be one of them," he said, firmer this time. "Look, I know you think you have it all figured out, but be sensible, Winnie, we're talking about a child. Our child. Don't you want the best for him or her?"

"Of course I do," she retorted.

He waved a hand to their surroundings. "And a one-bedroom apartment above a bakery is the best? I don't think so."

Her temper quickly flared. "Well, I didn't plan on raising the baby here. I'll get a new place. A house, with a yard and a fence."

His brows came up and she knew what that meant. "And how do you propose to pay the rent on a bigger place? With good intentions?"

Winona fought to keep her temper in check. "You can be so obnoxious when you want to be," she said and jumped to her feet. "Do you think I haven't spent the last few days thinking about how I'm going to do this? I've been thinking about Regina's offer to buy into the bakery. Until then, I plan on taking on more hours at the tourist center and I have a little nest egg saved. Not much," she added when she saw his brows shoot up again. "But enough that I won't be relying on good intentions to feed and clothe my child.

Anyway, I don't want to talk to you when you're in one of these moods."

"I'm not in a mood," he said quietly. "I just want to work this out."

Winona stalked across the room and opened the door. "For the record, you are the last man on earth I want to be married to."

Of course it was a lie. But he'd never know that.

"Too late," he said and tucked the envelope under his arm, "because you *are* married to me, Winnie. Remember that while you're trying to stay mad at me for believing this is the best solution for everyone."

She closed the door loudly behind him, stormed across the room and waited by the window, watching as he got into his car and drove off. He was being impossible. And absurd. They couldn't stay married for the sake of the baby.

Winona sunk down in the love seat and pressed her fingers to her temple. The last couple of weeks had been the most confusing of her life. She glanced at the collection of framed photos on the sideboard. There were a couple of her with her grandfather, another with Ellie and Leah and a couple of herself with Grant. She focused on her favorite one, taken a few years earlier at the spring fair. They were sharing a seat on the Ferris wheel; his arm was loped across her shoulders and she had one hand against his chest. They were laughing, heads close together, her hair whipping around them. She'd loved the selfie so much she had it printed and framed. Grant had the identical picture in his apartment.

And as loath as she was to admit it, she knew that Grant was right—she couldn't raise a child on good intentions. She had some savings, having spent a portion of her little nest egg on a wedding dress and a gaudy hotel room, leaving less than three thousand dollars in her checking account. She did plan on asking for more hours at the tourist center, and talking to Regina about the bakery. At least she had some time to save up and get a new place, and of course she'd stay in town.

She was tidying her herb rack in the kitchen late that afternoon when her cell pealed. It was Grant.

"What do you want?" she asked sharply.

"You were angry earlier," he said calmly. "I'm just making sure you're okay. That *we're okay.*"

"I'm fine," she said.

"Can I see you tonight?"

"No," she replied. "Where are you? At the ranch?"

"Outside O'Sullivan's," he said, "planning on getting takeout. Abby's working tonight and said she'd make risotto. Can I bring you some?" He paused. "Please, Winnie, I really don't want to leave things like that between us."

His words faltered her resistance and she made an irritated sound. "Okay, but you can't stay long."

"Just dinner, I promise."

She hung up. Forty minutes later he was back on her doorstep, leaning one shoulder against the jamb, carrying a bag of food. She was hungry, and for a second, as she took in how good he looked in low-rise jeans and a white polo, she wasn't sure what she was hungrier for—dinner or Grant. She swallowed hard, ignoring her weakening will, and let him inside.

"That smells good," she said as she inhaled.

He grinned. "Luckily my sister-in-law is the head chef at the best restaurant in town."

Winona grabbed plates and set the table. "What did you do this afternoon?"

"Drove around," he admitted. "Avoided my family like the plague."

She sat down and dished out their dinner. "So, you haven't told anyone?"

"No," he replied. "I'm not quite sure what I'd say at this point."

"Well, we probably shouldn't say anything until I reach the second trimester," she said, voicing something she'd been considering all day. "Just to be sure."

"Are you worried?" he asked, looking uncharacteristically uncomfortable. "I mean, that you might lose the baby?"

"No," she replied. "It's just a precaution. Once I go to the doctor I'll know more. I'll probably get vitamins and brochures on pregnancy—the usual."

"There's a usual?" he asked and shrugged. "You seem relaxed about it. I envy that. I'm way out of my comfort zone."

"I'm not relaxed," she admitted. "I'm faking it.

But I've had a couple of days to get used to the idea. Plus, once I skipped my period, I had my suspicions, so I was semiprepared for the test results. And actually, you seem pretty calm right now. Did you sign the divorce papers?"

"No," he replied. "I had other things on my mind."

"What?" she asked. "Your loveless marriage idea?"

He sat back in the chair, watching her intently. "It wouldn't be loveless. We care about each other."

He cared. Of course Winona knew he loved her, she'd never doubted it. But it wasn't enough. She wanted more from marriage. She wanted everything.

"There's a big difference between *loving* someone and being *in love*, Grant."

"Is there?" he shot back with a loose shrug. "Maybe there's not. Maybe it's all the same and we just have this insatiable need to put a label on it. I'm sure there are marriages that have started out with a lot less."

"Probably," she remarked. "But I'm not prepared to sell out. And you shouldn't be, either, just because you don't believe in romantic love."

"I don't think that."

"Sure you do," she said and pushed some risotto around on her plate. "Do you remember when I fell for Callum McCrae in senior year? You told me I had sawdust in my eyes and that it was merely simple chemistry. Just lust. Desire. Sex. And that being *in love* was a fantasy."

"He was a jerk, anyway," Grant said and scowled.

"Maybe. The thing is, I know there's a difference...and that doesn't make me a schmuck. It takes guts to fall in love. And yeah, when it doesn't work out it hurts like hell, but that isn't going to stop me and the rest of the world from trying to find it."

Grant didn't want to waste any energy remembering the guy she'd had the hots for in high school. By then he was graduating college and planning his future. Winona falling for some jock Grant never thought was good enough for her was a distraction he hadn't needed back then.

"He was your first boyfriend," Grant said and realized he'd spoken out loud.

She regarded him curiously, her brown eyes darkening. "He was my first everything. First kiss. First..." She blushed.

"You lost your virginity to him in the back seat of his pickup," he reminded her, and wasn't sure why the memory sat like cement in his stomach. "Classy guy."

Her mouth curled at the edges. "I called you that night, remember? You gave me a lecture about birth control. Ironic, really, considering the way things have worked out."

Heat crawled up his neck. "You were a girl back then. Now you're a woman. And I never liked the guy."

"You didn't like Dwight, either. Look, I know

you were only trying to protect me," she said quietly. "And still are in your own way. But you don't have to be a hero here, Grant. Plenty of people co-parent children without being married."

"But we *are* married, Winnie," he said. "There's the difference. And we should tell your grandfather the truth as soon as possible."

"I would prefer—"

"I'm not good at pretending. Or lying, even if it's by omission."

He watched as her expression grew taut. "What will people think?"

"I don't much care," he replied. "I care about what you think. What I think. I care about doing what's right. I care about my family."

"They'll be shocked."

He shrugged loosely. "So, what? Let them be shocked—they'll get over it. The only thing we can control is how we respond to things. I'm not going to let you raise this child alone when I can do something about it. I'm not going to see you living in a tiny apartment when I can afford to buy us a house." He put his hand up when she opened her mouth to retaliate. "I know you think this is me being bossy... but it's not. It's me being sensible and pragmatic and a more honorable kind of father than my own ever was. I won't shirk my responsibility to you or our baby. Call me old-fashioned, call me anything you like, but I'm not walking away."

He felt better once he'd said it, once she knew exactly how he felt about the situation.

By now their dinner had turned cold and she looked as though her appetite had gone with it. Grant pushed both their plates aside and reached for her hand, grasping the edge of her fingers and linking them with his own. They stayed like that for a moment, gazes connected, fingers touching, ignoring everything else in the room and the rest of the world.

Finally, she pulled her hand away. "We've been friends a long time, Grant, so I'm not about to rush and make a decision that will impact the rest of our lives. We have plenty of time to work out how we want to co-parent this baby. Plenty of time to figure out how we want to manage…*us*. Until then, I think we need to go through with the divorce and try to get our lives in order."

He saw the resolute determination in her expression and suspected he'd lost a round, despite his impassioned speech about doing the right thing. Winnie was as stubborn as a mule when she wanted to be, so making demands wasn't going to work. He had to get her to see that staying married was the best option—even if he wasn't really sure what that would look like.

He shrugged agreeably. "We'll take things slowly. But I won't compromise in one area."

"Which one?" she asked suspiciously.

"Telling your grandfather, and my family. I'm a hopeless secret keeper, you know that," he said and offered a rueful grin. "It will feel too much like a lie and I've got enough secrets going on with the whole Billie-Jack situation. So, compromise…yes?"

She exhaled, taking her time, and then shrugged. "All right," she agreed. "We'll tell them soon."

"I'm heading back to Rapid City tomorrow, and Friday I'm traveling to Denver and will be there for about five days. A company conference," he added when she regarded him curiously. "You know, building team morale and that kind of thing."

"Oh, Krystal will have you all to herself for five days."

He had no idea why she said it. Or why her voice sounded like she was having an attack of jealousy. Normally she laughed about it. But she wasn't laughing at that moment. She looked lethally serious. It sparked something inside him—something he couldn't define.

"What?"

"Nothing," she said quickly. "Ignore me."

"I can stay if you're worried about it."

She shook her head. "I'm not worried. And I know you have the kind of job that involves traveling and conferences and things like that."

He still wasn't convinced she was okay with the idea. "It's just for five days. How about we tell everyone when I get back?"

She got to her feet and cleared the plates. "Sure, if that's what you want… I may as well endure complete humiliation in one fell swoop."

It sounded like an insult, as though being married to him and carrying his baby was the worst possible scenario imaginable. Sure, he hadn't been expecting it, but she didn't have to make it sound like it was a life comparable to being slung into the depths of hell.

He stood up and pulled his keys from his pocket. "Are you working tomorrow?"

"I have a short shift that starts at two."

He nodded. "I'll call you in the morning."

"What for?"

His gaze dropped to her flat belly. "Just to say hi—isn't that reason enough?"

She sighed and then nodded. "I guess. Good night, Grant."

"Night, Winnie." He hesitated. "Sweet dreams."

It's not what he wanted to say…nowhere near it. He wanted to tell her everything would be okay. That they'd work through it together. That they were unbreakable. But the promises got stuck in his throat.

He left her apartment quickly, taking his mood with him, although he didn't go straight back to the ranch. He took a detour to Joss's house. His brother owned a big brick-and-tile place on a leafy, peaceful street not too far from town and he pulled up outside. It was after eight and by the time he got to the porch the overhead light flicked on and his brother was at the door.

"Hey," Joss said agreeably, his blondish hair shimmering under the light. "What's up? You looking for a place to crash?"

Grant crossed the threshold. "No, I'm staying at

the ranch tonight. I just thought I'd stop by for a while. Are the girls asleep?"

Joss chuckled. "At eight o'clock? No. But they are in their rooms and probably won't surface for the rest of the evening since it's a school night. I was just about to do some ironing."

Grant followed his brother down the long hallway and into the kitchen. "Sounds like a wild night ahead."

His brother laughed again. "I reserve my wild nights for every second weekend when the girls go to the in-laws' place."

Grant spotted the ironing board set up and a huge basket of clean laundry on the table. The kitchen was spotless, with everything where it should be, and his admiration for his brother amplified. Joss was one of those people who managed to be good at everything. He had a successful business, owned several rental properties in town, was raising two girls and seemed to juggle his entire life without any hiccups.

"You make all of this look easy," Grant remarked as he accepted the beer his brother passed him. "How do you do it?"

"It's not easy," Joss replied. "But I have to keep it together for the kids, you know. They were so young when Lara passed away, and this is all they know now. Routine is the key. So, what's up?"

Grant took a long breath. "Billie-Jack contacted me."

It wasn't what he intended to say. It wasn't even close. He wasn't even sure he'd planned on saying anything. He also wasn't sure why he'd stopped by his brother's place. Usually he tackled things on his own—particularly girl trouble. Although this wasn't the kind of trouble he'd ever found himself in before. But a niggling sense of loyalty to Winnie kept him from saying anything about the convoluted state of their relationship in that moment. It was best he talked about something else—like their father.

"Son of a bitch!" Joss said and shook his head. "What the hell does he want?"

"I don't know. He called my cell a few weeks back and I haven't replied to his message."

His brother scowled. "How the hell did he find your number?"

"I don't know that, either. I guess he probably looked me up online. Let's face it, tracking someone down these days is not hard."

Joss took a long swallow of beer and rested his behind on the counter. "You gonna call him back?"

"I'm not sure what I'm going to do," Grant replied. "I suppose I'm curious, but I also know that it's kind of like disturbing a hornet's nest."

"Ain't that the truth. Do yourself a favor," Joss warned. "Don't tell Jake. Or Hank. And for God's sake, don't say anything to Mitch. Or Ellie," he added with a rueful expression. "You know how she gets when anyone mentions Billie-Jack."

Grant exhaled heavily. He did know. Ellie had a load of unresolved resentment for their father, like he did. But out of all of them, he suspected Ellie was the one who had the most abandonment issues—especially since she could barely remember their mother.

"That's why I'm telling *you*," Grant said and grinned.

Joss looked at him seriously. "Maybe he wants money."

"It's possible. Or he could want to make amends. Neither is out of the question. Eighteen years is a long time."

"Smart move on the old man's part, though," Joss said quietly. "Contacting you first."

"Smart? How?"

"Because you're the most sensible one out of all of us. Jake and Ellie can be hotheads, Mitch is overprotective, I'm too cynical and of course Hank has every reason to hate the guy until the end of time. Whereas you are perfectly reasonable and levelheaded. You don't screw up anything. Freakin' annoying, really," Joss said and laughed a little.

Grant almost laughed back. Almost. But he couldn't stop thinking about Joss's words. Reasonable and levelheaded. Someone who never screws up in life. It made him sound as dull as an old shoe. But he figured it wasn't too way off the mark…mostly. For all everyone knew, he was the guy who got his act together when he was a teenager, studied hard, was valedictorian in high school, finished college with honors and had his pick of top employers when he graduated. He'd never gotten a speeding ticket, never spent a night in jail, never did drugs. Yeah…he was levelheaded, all right.

Except for the situation he was now in.

Grant stayed for a while longer, talking mostly about Billie-Jack, and he listened to his brother's sage advice. He said goodbye around nine, lingering by the bottom step off the porch.

Hell, everything was such a mess.

"You know," he said as he kicked at a pebble on the path. "I do screw up sometimes."

Joss regarded him curiously. "You do?"

He nodded. Then, realizing Joss couldn't see his expression in the darkness, he sighed and said. "Sure. Big-time."

"Like what?"

Guilt pushed down on his shoulders. "Nothing… forget I said anything."

Joss stepped forward. "Not likely. What's going on?"

He made a self-derisive sound, the words suddenly tumbling out. "A couple of weeks back I went to Vegas with Winnie because she was going to elope with that marine. He didn't show up. So instead, we got drunk, got married, spent the night together and now she's pregnant," he announced, his voice sounding hollow as it carried on the breeze. "Oh, and even though she's having my baby, she still wants to go ahead with the divorce. How's that for a screwup?"

Joss teetered on the edge of the top step. "You're serious?"

"Yep."

"Holy crap. I take back what I said. That's a big pile of trouble you got there."

"The biggest of my life," he admitted.

"If she's having your kid, why does she want a divorce?" Joss asked the obvious question.

"Because she doesn't want to be married to me. She went to Vegas to marry the marine, remember?"

"She still loves him, then," Joss said, voicing what Grant had been stewing silently on all day.

"I guess," he replied flatly. "People don't just switch off, right? Anyway, keep the news to yourself, will you? We were hoping to tell the family and Red together, this weekend. And I promised Winnie I wouldn't say a word, and here I just spilled my guts to you."

"I won't say anything," Joss replied. "Discretion is my middle name. Take care of yourself. And call me if you need me."

Grant nodded as he turned and walked down the path, through the gate and back to his car. He was halfway back into town when he decided against crashing at the ranch for the night, and instead headed for the hotel. He was checked in, showered and trying to sleep by ten o'clock.

Despite the turmoil of his dreams, he actually had a better night than the previous one cramped up on Winnie's couch, and managed to get a run in early the following morning. Afterward, he ordered room service and tried to ignore the niggling thoughts going through his mind.

She still loves him...

He had no idea why his brother's words were hanging around in his head. The marine was history. But since she'd told Grant point-blank that he was the last man she wanted to be married to, he wondered if she was still thinking about her ex-fiancé. She'd pretty much said she was over Dwight...but how could he be sure?

The whole situation was messed up...but he had to fix it, to make it right, to get Winnie to see that staying married was the best solution. So yeah, maybe he hadn't imagined he'd be married with a baby on the way a few weeks back, but since he was, there was no turning back. He had to step up and do what was right. They both did. A Culhane did not turn his back on family and responsibility. If he did, he'd be no better than Billie-Jack—and that wasn't a legacy he intended carrying on.

He rummaged through the side pocket in his overnight bag and found the wedding band he'd ripped off so quickly a couple of weeks earlier. So much had happened since then. He stared at the ring, thinking about the simple significance of the small circle. And knew instantly what he had to do.

He was back on her doorstep by nine, and when she answered the door she almost looked as though she'd been expecting him.

"I'm not staying, I promise," he assured her and exhaled. "But please, let me say something."

"What?" she asked, looking as though she'd had very little sleep.

"I know this isn't our idea of an ideal situation. But here we are, together," he reminded her and saw her wince. "So, we need to take a breath and think about what this really means for our future and our child's future. Family…" he said, his words trailing off as he fought the urge to take her hands, to connect with her, to make her see that their child was worth fighting for. "You were right when you said I've never really thought about getting married. Or having kids. But you're my best friend, Winnie, and the fact is we're also husband and wife. And I can't believe we're not going to try to make this work. I believe we care about each other enough to at least give it a shot, don't you?"

The color leached from her face and she crossed her arms tightly. "Marriage is—"

"Not final," he said quietly. "We both know that. And since we've got eight or so months until the baby comes, we've got time to try and figure it out." He lifted his left hand and fiddled with the wedding band that was now back on his finger. "I'm going to wear this from now on, or at least until we know for sure that being married isn't something we can do. Because I don't know that for sure. Neither do you. This might turn out to be the best thing that happens to either of us."

"Or the worst," she added.

"Maybe," he said and shrugged loosely. "But you

know what I don't want to do, Winnie? I don't want to look into the eyes of our son or daughter when he or she is born, or on a first birthday, or a tenth birthday, or graduation, or wedding day, and admit that we didn't give it a chance. That we bailed because we were scared to fail or afraid of commitment or were pining after something or someone else or thinking of some foolishly romantic ideal about what a successful marriage looks like. If we screw up, at least we screw up without excuses. Please say you'll consider it?"

He grasped her hand and urged her close, holding her against him, and she came willingly, looking up at him, her brown eyes wide and warm. And he kissed her. Not hot and heavy. Now wasn't the time for that. It was a simple, almost chaste kiss, just their mouths fleetingly together, tasting each other for a few moments.

When he pulled back and lifted his head, she was breathing hard, still looking at him. "Okay," she said softly. "I'll think about it."

Grant released her and stepped back. "I'll call you."

"Don't," she replied. "I need some time to sort this out in my head. I hear what you're saying, Grant, and a part of me knows you're right. But I *am* scared. And confused. Things used to be so simple between us and now everything is completely different. This is a new reality for us both. And even though you might think it's okay if we screw it up, I'm not really wired that way. I need to be sure."

The thing was, Grant thought as he left, they both knew there were no guarantees.

Chapter Seven

Winona spent the next week in varying states of indecision. Grant didn't call her. He texted, though, asking how she was, keeping the messages brief and lighthearted. She responded each time with a simple emoji, not wanting to get bogged down with more conversation, more explanation, more...anything. And she made it her mission to not think about the Krystal factor. He'd told her plenty of times that he wasn't interested in the other woman and she had no reason to disbelieve him. The only thing she couldn't believe was her own reaction.

She also avoided the world for the following days, hanging low, taking on extra hours at the tourist center over the weekend to avoid Ellie's invitation to go horse riding at the ranch. She even bailed on her catching up with her grandfather, pleading a headache and promising to drop by the ranch soon. On Monday she went to her doctor's appointment and her pregnancy was officially confirmed. She was given a list of vitamins and supplements to take, and the name of an obstetrician in Rapid City. The community hospital in Cedar River had a good birthing unit and she took down those details, as well.

And she thought about Grant…a lot. Some days it seemed that he was *all* she thought about.

She thought about their last conversation and tried to make it right in her head.

Stay married. Be married. Try to make it work. Do the right thing.

And that kiss. A kiss that had her yearning for her secret dreams. A kiss that reminded her of everything they weren't. A kiss so sweet it held the promise of more…but she knew in her heart that he didn't have more to give.

He turned up on her doorstep on Thursday morning, dressed in cargoes, a pale gray shirt and dress shoes. She gestured to his overnight bag. "Are you planning on moving in?"

He shrugged. "Gotta start sometime."

"That's presumptuous. I haven't given you my answer."

He walked into the room and sat on one of the kitchen stools. "I know. I guess I was hoping you might've had some time to think about things and maybe make a decision."

"I *have* made a decision," she said. "And you can sleep on the couch."

His mouth twisted. "Now who's being presumptuous?"

"Just keeping things manageable," she said and glanced at his left hand, spotting the gold ring instantly. "I bet that put a dampener on any hooking-up opportunities this week."

His brows shot up. "Is that what's been keeping you up these nights, Winnie? Worried that your brand-new husband was straying?" He laughed, but there was little humor in his tone. "Rest assured, I was not. You know me better than that."

She did. He wasn't a cheat or a liar. He was the most honest man she knew. And she immediately felt foolish for saying it, let alone allowing herself to wallow in the idea for the previous few days. And he was right about the other thing, too—she had made a decision…perhaps the biggest of her life.

"We'll try this marriage thing for sixty days," she announced, arms crossed, her heart almost in her throat.

"Sixty days?"

"That's how long it takes to get a divorce, right?"

"Yes," he replied and scowled. "So let me get this straight. You want to sign the divorce papers and *then* try to make this relationship work? That doesn't make a whole lot of sense."

"It does to me. By then we'll definitely know if we've done the right thing or not in plenty of time before the baby arrives."

"So, we go into this with our expectations as low as possible, correct?"

It sounded like a coward's compromise, but Winona wasn't prepared to commit to anything more. She didn't share his confidence that they could make it work. And she knew why. Grant had a barbed-wire fence around his heart. He looked at it purely from an economical point of view. They had a baby coming, they were already married—presto, problem solved.

But she...she was different.

She tucked her tote in her lap. "Well, if we *can* make it work, we'll have enough time to stop the divorce going through."

"Well, since I'm not in any real position to make demands, sure."

Winona nodded. "Thank you. Although maybe we should postpone today and—"

"Winnie, I told Joss last week," he admitted guiltily. "I'm sorry, I know I said we'd wait until I got back. But I needed..."

His words trailed off, but she knew what he was going to say. He needed to talk to someone. And it pained her. Because up until a few weeks ago, she would have been his go-to person. Now their relationship seemed to be altering daily. Every time they spoke, the tension between them grew. Tension that was manifested from all angles.

"I understand," she said, thinking she needed her own confidante, and experienced an acute rush of loneliness. "Although I think I should be the one who tells my grandfather," she said.

"Maybe we should do it together."

"And then?" she asked. "After we've told everyone, what then? You said you were staying for a few days…and afterward?"

"House hunting, I guess. We can stop by the Realtor in town and check out some places."

"Move in together right away? That's your great plan?"

He looked at her and nodded. "Married people usually live together, Winnie. There's no point in making it some soft transition." He glanced around the apartment. "And there's not a lot to pack here."

"What about your place in Rapid City?" she inquired.

"I can find a tenant," he replied quietly.

"Well. If you're sure it won't be too hard to find someone, I guess it's settled. So, how was your conference?" she asked, changing the subject. "Did you get plenty of team building done?"

He shrugged. "It was fine."

"Normally we talk about it," she reminded him.

"Normally we do, yes. But you don't seem like you're in the mood for chitchat," he said quietly.

"I always want to hear about your work stuff," she said and smiled a little.

He did the same. "Well, then, yeah, it was okay.

Just a typical work conference. Interesting meetings, crappy buffet and some attendees drank too much. Nothing out of the ordinary. We should get going."

"And the Krystal factor?"

His brows rose questioningly. "She was mostly well behaved."

Winona scowled and smiled. "Well, she's only human and you can be very charming."

He laughed. "Do you think? I thought I drove you crazy?"

"We were discussing Krystal, not me. But since we've decided to try and make this marriage work, I'm glad she kept her hands to herself."

"You know, fidelity's not a huge price to pay," he remarked.

It seemed an odd comment, but she didn't dwell on it.

When they got to the Triple C, Winona waited for him and they walked toward Red's cottage together. As expected, her grandfather was delighted to see her, and happy to see Grant, too.

She hugged him for longer than usual, and once they were seated she took a deep breath and spoke, her hands shaking so badly she pressed them into her thighs. "Papa... I've got something to tell you."

"*We've* got something to tell you," Grant corrected gently and grabbed her left hand, holding it within his.

Strength seeped through her and she nodded, taking another galvanizing breath. "Well, the thing is, a few weeks ago…we… Grant and I, we…eloped."

"Eloped?" Red echoed.

She nodded. "Yes, Papa, we got married."

Grant cleared his throat a little. "We know it seems…sudden. And we probably should have spoken to you about it. But we're going to get a place in town, so Winnie won't be far away from you."

Winona waited for her grandfather to respond, and when he did, Red's face creased with a smile. "Well, congratulations. I'm thrilled for you two."

She nodded and swallowed hard. "Ah…there's something else."

Red's eyes seemed to twinkle. "More good news?"

Grant squeezed her hand gently, and she nodded. "We think so. You're going to be a great-grandfather, Papa. I'm having a baby."

"Damn," Red said and clapped his hands together. "That's just wonderful."

In a way, he almost seemed relieved, as though some great burden had been lifted from his shoulders. She didn't want to read too much into it, or overthink his reaction, as she was prone to do. He shook Grant's hand and congratulated them both again and, oddly, didn't ask too many questions about their plans, their intentions or anything else. He actually seemed to accept the marriage as a done deal. He said he was looking forward to being a great-grandfather and nodded agreeably when Grant said he would make sure she and the baby were cared for.

"That was easier than I thought it would be," she remarked as they walked toward the main house. "Too easy. He almost seemed relieved."

Grant chuckled. "Well, I'm clearly quite the catch."

She jabbed his ribs with her elbow. "Don't you think it's odd that he wasn't…I don't know…surprised?"

"We've known each other forever," he said and smiled. "It's not such a big stretch, is it?"

"How about the fact that you treat me like an annoying little sister?"

He stopped walking, grabbed her hand and brought her close to him, linking their fingertips. "Annoying best friend, maybe," he corrected. "But believe me, Winnie, there's nothing remotely brotherly about my feelings for you right now."

Winona looked up, her eyes wide as they met his. They were so close she could feel the heat coming off his skin. His cologne swirled around her, an intoxicating blend of spice and sea, and she shuddered a little too breathlessly. The pulse in his cheek throbbed as his irises darkened. A flash of memory assailed her, thinking about Vegas, about the way he lay above her that night, his weight on his elbows, their gazes connected with the same intense intimacy as their bodies. She remembered his kiss, the taste of him, the way his mouth and hands had explored her, the way she'd sighed and moaned and experienced pleasure so acute it was impossible to stop the heady flush rising up her neck. She remembered touching his face, his shoulders, his back. She remembered clinging to him, feeling every part of him against her, lifting her hips to meet his, pleading, urging, whispering words she'd never dared imagine she would have the chance to say.

"Winnie," he said quietly, one hand reaching up to touch her cheek. "For the sake of my sanity, can you please ditch the X-rated look in your eyes?"

She inhaled sharply. "I didn't mean to—"

"I know," he said, cupping her jaw as he softly sliced through her words. "This is all rather unexpected, isn't it?"

"This?"

The pressure of his touch increased a fraction and he traced his finger down her neck. "The foggy brain that comes from having sex with someone."

She smiled, knowing exactly what he meant. Yes, *foggy brain* certainly described how she was feeling.

"Hey, you two!"

It was Ellie, her voice ringing out clearly from where she stood on the veranda. Grant released Winona immediately and she turned, ignoring Ellie's curious expression as she climbed the steps.

"Hey, Brat," Grant said affectionately. "Mitch and Tess around?"

Ellie nodded. "What's going on?"

"Come inside and find out," he said and ushered Winona into the house.

His brother and sister-in-law greeted them in the

hallway and moments later they were all in the living room, talking to and over each other as usual. Winona had the urge to hold his hand, to seek comfort, protection. Then she scolded herself. She didn't need protecting from the Culhanes. They were friends. *Family.* They would understand. Winona looked at them all amid the hubbub, noticing how Tess was watching her with a tiny smile on her face, almost as though she had guessed their news before the words were spoken.

It took Grant about ten seconds to break the news of their situation, so matter-of-factly it was over before she realized.

"Winnie and I got married and we're having a baby," he said before he looked at her, offered a reassuring nod and waited for a response.

"You're what?"

It was Ellie who spoke first, Ellie who was regarding them incredulously.

"Married," Grant said again, looking as cool as always. "And having a baby."

Winona wished she had his calm demeanor. She did have a tendency to let her feelings show in her expression, and she suspected this was one of those times.

"This is rather sudden, isn't it?" Mitch asked, looking at them both in turn.

Grant shrugged. "It is what it is."

Ellie was on her feet, clearly not buying it. "I

don't understand. Where does Dwight fit into this little scenario?"

"He doesn't," Winona replied, looking at her friend and seeing the disbelief in her expression. "We broke up."

"And now you're married to my brother and having a baby?" Ellie asked, brows up, clearly suspicious. "Oh, my gosh, is it Dwight's?"

"Settle down, Ellie," Grant said and perched on the edge of the sofa. "Stop jumping to conclusions. It's my—"

"It's Grant's baby," Winona said, her tone unequivocal, and she stood, straightening her back. "If you want details, I *had* planned to elope with Dwight in Vegas," she admitted, heat coursing through her veins. "But he was a no-show. He dumped me. Your brother was there to walk me down the aisle, but instead we got drunk together, got married and had sex. Now I'm pregnant. And seeing as I hadn't seen Dwight for ten months, you do the math."

"Couldn't have said it better myself," Grant added and got up, grasping her hand. "Look, we're not asking for approval or advice. It's done. We're married. We're having a baby. What we choose to do from now on is our business. What we would like, though, is for you to share in the good news."

"You must have expected us to be surprised," Ellie said, still looking suspicious.

It was Tess who spoke next... Tess who was the calm voice among the building family chaos.

"Congratulations. Babies are always a wonderful way to bring people together. We should have a celebration," she suggested and smiled. "A post-wedding get-together for the whole family. How about I arrange something for next weekend? Ellie would love to help me, wouldn't you?" she asked and grasped Ellie's hand.

Ellie was quickly agreeing and a minute later the date was set for the following Sunday for a relaxing gathering at the ranch, with family and close friends.

"Are you moving to Rapid City?" Mitch asked Winona.

"I'm moving back to Cedar River," Grant supplied. "We'll look at getting a place on the north side of town to cut down my commute. But I'm doing so much interstate work at the moment, it's not imperative that I live in Rapid City."

"You'd be welcome to move back to the ranch," Mitch offered. "I suspect Red would love having you close by, Win."

"Thank you," she said and managed a smile, thinking that the last thing she wanted was for her relationship with Grant to be under some kind of Culhane sibling microscope, as much as she cared about them all. "But we really—"

"We appreciate the offer," Grant interjected, taking the heat off her in the process. "Thanks a lot. But I think we need our own space for the time being."

"Your brother is right," Winona said gently. "We

have a lot to adjust to—and a lot to get ready for. And you guys know that better than anyone."

Mitch and Tess smiled at each other, then Mitch turned back to his brother. "I guess that's true enough."

They left shortly afterward, after hugs and handshakes and the promise to be in touch about the family catch-up on the following weekend. Once they were in the car, she spoke up.

"Ellie went all lioness," she said and actually managed a grin. "Thinking I've trapped you into marriage with another man's baby."

"My sister is a drama queen," Grant said as they drove through the gates. "Still, she knows me pretty well."

"What do you mean?"

"That if you needed someone to raise a child with, I would do it."

Winona sucked in a breath. Because, despite everything, of course she knew that about him. He would slay her dragons if need be. "But you *know* this baby is yours, right? I mean, I would never expect you to—"

"I know," he said and grasped her hand. "And I'm not unhappy about the baby, Winnie. I'm still in a kind of shock," he added and grinned, "but have accepted the idea."

"Resigned to it, you mean? And to your upcoming sixty days in purgatory?"

"You're the one who set the time frame, remember?"

"I need a plan," she said and pulled free, placing both hands in her lap. "And honestly, since you usually like things organized and in order, I'd imagine a workable plan with a time frame and parameters would be right up your ally."

"Ah," he said and turned off onto the highway. "Now come the terms and conditions."

Winona huffed. "What's gotten into you? Of course we need ground rules. Firstly, we need to promise to always be honest with each other."

"I thought we already did that," he said. "But if you're asking for assurances, then how about we talk about the marine."

"Dwight? What does he have to do with this?"

"You tell me," he shot back as they drove toward town. "A month ago he was the love of your life and all you ever wanted."

She wasn't sure she'd ever said that. And the truth was, she'd barely spared Dwight a thought over the last couple of weeks. "That was before he dumped me at the altar and I got married to someone else," she reminded him, hearing something off in his tone and not quite sure what to make of it. "I haven't heard from Dwight since that day and I don't expect to ever again."

His hands were tight on the steering wheel. "Okay, back to these ground rules—what's next?"

Winona stared straight ahead, seeing the town's welcome sign. "Well, I think we should *rent* a house first, in case things don't work out. And I don't think we should...you know...sleep together."

Grant pulled the car into a spot outside the Realtor's office. He didn't say a word as they headed inside and met with the owner, Leola Jurgens, who quickly detailed to them all the available rental listings. Grant was more interested in buying property, but he wasn't about to get into an argument with Winnie about it. She had her mind set firmly on renting a place. It seemed like she had her mind firmly set on a lot of things. Like not sharing a bed. Sure, he hadn't committed to this arrangement specifically with sex on the brain—but he hadn't bargained on *not* sleeping with his wife, either.

They made appointments to look at two homes the following day, after Winnie finished her morning shift at work. As they were leaving the Realtor's, she said she wanted to stop by the supermarket. They lingered in the store for a while and Grant added things to the shopping cart he knew she'd turn her nose up at—like alfalfa sprouts and avocado. Winnie was more a meat-and-potatoes kind of girl.

They were climbing the stairs to her apartment, his arms loaded with grocery bags, when his cell rang. He shuffled the bags into one hand and pulled his phone from his pocket. It was a number he now recognized.

Billie-Jack.

His gut rolled and he fought the urge to pick up.

Now wasn't the time or place to have his first conversation with his father in eighteen years.

"Something wrong?" Winnie asked, clearly picking up on his expression.

"Billie-Jack. Again."

"Oh," she said and sighed. "You haven't called him back yet?"

"No. Although I did speak to Joss about it."

"What did he say?" she asked.

"To keep the information to myself," he replied and offered a wry smile. "Joss hates Billie-Jack."

"Do you?"

"I'm not sure how I feel," he said and placed the bags on the kitchen counter.

"If you want to see him, then you should."

"It's complicated," he said and watched as she began unpacking the groceries.

"Most relationships are," she said and waved a hand between them. "But you know him, you remember him. You know what he's like and who he is. And yes, perhaps he has changed. Or maybe not. Either way, at least you can go into it without risking being disappointed."

"It would be easier if he hasn't changed," Grant admitted. "Then I could just tell him to go to hell and to leave the family alone."

"And what if he has?" she asked. "Then what do you do?"

"Then I have to make a decision that's not only mine to make—because I was younger than my brothers, I didn't see the worst of him. I think I saw what I wanted to see."

"You were, what, six or seven when your mom died? It's natural that you would want to look to your father for stability and strength."

"Strength?" he echoed and gave a shallow laugh. "Yeah, I guess I did. Not that he showed any. He used to beat up on Joss and Hank and I remember how Jake would put himself in the middle of the fights to take the worst of it. But I still wanted his time, you know, I still wanted a father. By then the others had put up with so much of his crap that they were glad to see him go."

"But you weren't," she said, more statement than question. "But you were young, impressionable. Don't feel guilty because you wanted your dad to *be* a dad. That's a normal human need."

She had a point and he realized it was the first time they'd had a meaningful conversation about something *other* than the convoluted state of their own relationship for weeks.

"I'll do a better job than he did," Grant said and glanced at her belly. "I promise."

She nodded. "I know you will."

"It means a lot, you know," he said and rested on the counter, watching as she put the last of the items away. "That you think I can be a good dad. If I'm half the father that my brothers are, I'll get it right."

"Mitch is a good role model for fatherhood," she

said quietly. "He was, what—eighteen when your dad left?"

"Yeah. And Joss got married straight out of high school because he and Lara were pregnant. If they can do it at eighteen, I figure I can do it at thirty."

She smiled, a deep, warm smile that caught his breath and made his stomach dive. It occurred to him that he hadn't seen her smile much lately. And he'd missed it. In fact, he missed their comradery, and the sense of companionship they'd always shared.

"It's good to see you smiling," he remarked and moved around the counter. "So, how about you get out of the kitchen and let me make us a sandwich of champions."

Her mouth curled at the edges. "Okay, but no avocado."

"Where's your sense of adventure," he teased, stupidly happy that they were talking like normal and there was zero tension hanging between them. Or at least they were pretending there wasn't. "One semisandwich of champions coming up."

She chuckled. "So, what's your plan for the next few days?" she asked, changing the subject.

"I'll stay in town for the rest of the week. I have to get back to the office Monday and fly out Tuesday to Duluth for a couple of days—a group of us from the office are working on a project for a food manufacturing company. But I'll be back by the Friday, you know, in case we find a place and start moving."

She didn't blink. "Ah, I have a rental agreement

here, so I'll have to sort that out. And you said you were going to lease your apartment?"

Grant nodded and began preparing their food while she perched herself on a stool on the other side of the counter and entertained herself with her phone. It could have been any other day, he figured, with him in the kitchen and Winnie laughing at humorous memes she scrolled through on her social media accounts. She showed him a couple, laughing at a herd of baby goats wearing knitted pajamas and a meerkat lip-synching to a rap song.

"Promise me something," he said as he pushed a plate across the countertop.

She eyed the sandwich and then looked at him. "What?"

"That we'll always make each other laugh," he replied, feeling oddly serious.

She looked inside the sandwich, smiled when she saw he hadn't loaded it with ingredients she didn't like and nodded. "I promise. By the way, Leah's invited me to a party Saturday night. Would you like to come with me?"

Leah was his cousin and a good friend of Winnie's, too. Her mom, Sandra, was Billie-Jack's sister and had been killed in an airplane crash several years earlier, along with her daughter-in-law, Jayne. It had been a tough time for the family, but they had gotten through it with the help of many of their friends in town. Now, Leah was dating Sean O'Sullivan and they lived in a big house by the river. Grant liked

Leah, and her brother, David, was a good friend as well as being his cousin.

"Sure," he said agreeably. "We should start socializing together."

"We've been socializing together for years," she reminded him.

"I meant as a married couple," he said. "Not just best friends."

She blinked and shrugged. "Sure…whatever."

They stayed in her apartment for the remainder of the day. Grant set up his laptop on the desk near the window and did some work, while Winnie did laundry. Later, Grant cooked pasta for dinner and afterward they watched television for a while. The whole evening was absurdly domestic…until Winnie dumped a pillow and blanket on the end of the sofa around ten o'clock and disappeared into her room with a vague good night.

He was irritated about being relegated to the couch—but bit his tongue. They had enough problems without adding fuel to any more.

As he tossed on the couch for the next hour or so, Grant figured he should have checked into the hotel again. Or gone to the ranch. Either would have meant he'd get some sleep. He was still awake by eleven-thirty and headed to the kitchen to make herbal tea. He was grabbing a mug from the cupboard when Winnie unexpectedly came out from her room.

"Sorry," he said. "Did I wake you?"

"Couldn't sleep," she replied and rubbed her eyes.

She wore a short white T-shirt that was almost translucent with the light shining from the hallway. He swallowed hard, averted his gaze and got back to his task. "Tea?"

"Sure," she replied and came into the kitchen.

Her feet were bare and her toenails painted some sparkly purple color. She had nice legs, he thought as he grabbed another mug. And cute feet. In fact, everything about Winnie was in perfect proportion.

"Why do you think we did it?" she asked, startling him back into looking at her face.

"What?"

"Got married. Had sex. Why do you think we did it?"

Grant stared at her. It was the first time she'd asked the question. Not the first time he'd thought it…but hell, he'd been thinking all kind of things lately. He'd been thinking things about Winnie that surprised him…shocked him actually. Like how perfectly smooth her skin was, or how her lips curled up at the edges when she smiled. And he remembered, too, that night in Vegas; even though they'd had way too much to drink, deep down the memories were acute. Polarizing. And, in a way, terrifying…because it forced him to regard her in ways he'd consciously avoided. As not just his best friend. But as a woman… vibrant, sexy, desirable—all the things he'd purposefully put out of his mind since they were teenagers because back then, of course, he'd had the usual lustful thoughts. Thinking about her like that now was confusing. But they were married with a baby on the way, so how could he *not* think about her?

"I'm not sure."

"I'm trying to figure it out in my mind, you know," she said, crossing her arms in a way that pushed her breasts upward and got him thinking that a white T-shirt was just about the sexiest thing he'd ever seen. "I know I was upset about Dwight and embarrassed by it all. I know we drank a lot…but we've been drinking together before and nothing has ever happened between us. Something changed that night."

"Does it matter so much?" he asked, tired of over-thinking everything.

"Yes," she replied. "Because we're married and I'm sleeping in there and you're on the couch."

"Your ground rules," he reminded her. "Remember?"

"I know," she said and exhaled almost painfully. "But we need them, don't you think? Okay," she conceded, "*I* need them. And of course I know it's not logical for two people who are married, and are going to try and *be* married, to not sleep together."

"Then why suggest it?"

She shrugged. "I'm scared, I guess."

Grant stilled and looked at her. "Of me?"

"Of this," she said and waved a hand between them. "Of being…of having…of sex… I know that probably sounds crazy since we've already done it, but I don't have sex casually. And I know you, Grant.

I know you only have casual relationships. And I don't want to be someone who is on a list of your casual hookups."

It was quite the accusation. And if it wasn't true, he might have been annoyed. But she was right. His list of hookups wasn't that long by some standards—but it was definitely casual. One, two, three dates was his usual style. A two-month involvement at the most. Commitment free. Danger free. But this was Winnie. His best friend.

His wife.

The woman carrying his child.

This was pure commitment.

"Being with you *is* different," he said quietly, not really sure why he said it but feeling the truth of it deep down.

Her brows rose up. "How do you know? How can we be sure?"

"Because I remember that night," he replied. "I remember kissing you, touching you. And yeah, maybe how it started is a little blurry, and we wouldn't have done it if not for that last batch of tequila shots, but we did…and it was really something."

"Was it?" she asked, her skin oddly pale beneath the kitchen light. "What if it was just the alcohol and the—"

"What's this really about, Winnie?" he asked, ditching the tea making to stand in front of her, seeing uncertainty in her expression.

She shook her head, swallowing hard. "How can

I know if you…if you really…you know, *feel* that way…"

"Feel what way?" he asked, seeing her expression look more pained with each passing second.

"You know what way," she replied quietly. "Attraction and desire. I don't want to be with someone who has to fake it."

Grant stepped forward and touched her shoulder. A simple gesture. One he'd done countless times. Meant to reassure and comfort. But her skin was warm beneath his fingers and touching her sent a fast message to that part of him he'd had under wraps around her. He quickly realized he wanted to kiss her. And more.

"There's nothing fake about this, Winnie."

She didn't look convinced. "You can say whatever you want, Grant, but it doesn't change the past. It doesn't change us. It doesn't change that we've never…that you've never looked at me as anything other than your best friend."

He touched her belly with the back of his hand— desperate, suddenly, to curve his hand over the safe place where their baby was growing. To feel their child. To feel Winnie.

"I'm pretty sure this disputes that idea," he said and everything he'd always thought—the rock-solid belief he'd held that he knew exactly who he was and what he wanted—had somehow become hazy. Because there was so much he didn't know…so much he couldn't be sure of. And it alarmed him down to the soles of his feet. Except for one thing—the undisputable fact that he was attracted to his wife.

"You want proof," he asked and took her hand, resting her palm against his chest. "That's my heart, beating like crazy because I'm this close to you. Because I do want you...very much."

Chapter Eight

Winona knew what she was asking him. For the truth. For assurances. To know that if they were going to try and make their marriage work, he had to at least be honest about his feelings.

About sex.

Because she'd been battling her insecurities for days, demanding ground rules, and knowing it was foolish to expect a sexless relationship. Because she didn't want that, either. But what she really didn't want was to think of Grant making love to her when he had no real feelings for her in that regard. Sure, his heart might be pounding…but was that enough? She knew him—although he didn't do commitment, he wasn't indiscriminate and didn't hook up simply because he could. Like Krystal, she thought—who'd been giving him the eye for months and who he'd turned down because he wasn't interested in her. That made him a good guy, right? Someone with integrity and character. Someone she could depend on to be faithful and loyal.

She knew he loved her. Oh, not the passionate, soul mate kind of love, but he cared and with the baby coming, she hoped that would be enough. But sex was different. Sex was about physical intimacy and desire and she had no reason to believe he thought of her in that way—other than their drunken romp in a Vegas hotel room.

His expression was unrelenting and she inhaled sharply, relaxing a fraction. He touched her face with his free hand, cupping her cheek for a moment before gently anchoring her head so he could look directly into her eyes.

Grant dipped his head and touched his mouth to hers and her lips instantly parted beneath the soft pressure. He moved closer and her hands climbed up his chest to his shoulders, her fingers holding on, her breasts pressed against him. Heat rushed up her legs and into her belly, startling her with its ferocity as he deepened the kiss, finding her tongue and touching it with his own. She pressed closer, deeper, hotter, and for a moment all she could feel was his mouth and her hands and the erotic roll of her tongue against his. She'd been kissed before. She liked kissing. But nothing prepared her for the onslaught of feelings cascading through her blood, her bones, her very soul.

When he pulled back, putting a little space between them, her breath was coming out sharp and erratic. He stared at her, scanning her face, his gaze blisteringly intense.

"See…not fake," he said softly and stepped back, releasing her. "About as real as it gets."

She wanted to believe it. She *longed* to believe it. "Okay, so you kiss nice—it's not exactly proof that you're suddenly attracted to me."

He laughed softly, deeply, and the sound rumbled through her like an orchestra playing an adagio behind her ribs. "Suddenly? Is that what you think? Or don't think?"

"I think," she said and moved away a little, "that this is something of a novelty and at some point you're going to realize it's too much effort."

"You're being a little ridiculous, you know," he said and leaned back against the counter.

"Because I want honesty?"

"Because you want absolutes," he said and sighed. "And frankly, Winnie, I'm all out. Did I just wake up one morning and realize I thought of you as more than a friend? Well, no. We did something we wouldn't normally have done, in circumstances that were unusual, and that has somehow shifted the dynamic between us. I don't want to waste time wondering why. The truth is, I could easily ask you the same thing."

"That's different," she said hotly.

"Why?" he shot back. "Because I'm a man and we think about sex differently? You're right, maybe we do. Maybe you and I are absolutely on different pages here. But believe me, making love to you would not be an effort. Get some sleep," he said, suddenly sounding impatient. "We have appointments to see a few houses tomorrow."

Winona didn't linger, even though she felt like she was being scolded. She returned to her bedroom and closed the door. Sleep, of course, wasn't on the agenda, and she only managed to sneak in a few restless hours.

When she got out of bed at half past six, the apartment was empty and she figured Grant had gone for a run.

He returned around 7:15—hot, sweaty and as sexy as sin. By then, she'd already gone downstairs and grabbed a few things from the bakery for breakfast.

"Don't you ever cook breakfast?" he asked and looked at the strawberry cream-cheese bagel she'd placed on a plate.

"Not if I can help it," she replied. "I like to cook cakes and pies. You know that about me already."

"Well, it seems to matter more now that we're going to be living together. I gotta teach you how to eat something other than sweets," he said and shook his head.

She smiled übersweetly. "I suppose you'd prefer to raise our child on a vegetarian diet?"

"Would you object?" he asked.

Winona shrugged. "I can appreciate the benefits. But no kale juices, eggplant or avocado."

"Carnivore," he teased. "I'm going to take a shower."

"Don't use all the hot water," she warned, biting into her bagel.

"Join me, then?" he asked and pulled off his T-shirt. "For the sake of water consumption."

Winona rocked back on her heels and stared at his chest, almost choking on her mouthful of bagel. He really didn't have any right to look so good without clothes. It was too distracting. And all the talk about sex the night before had muddled her brain and she couldn't stop thinking about it. About him. About their future together as husband and wife.

"Is this flirting the new thing between us?" she asked, trying to keep her tone light.

"Why not," he replied and tossed the T-shirt over one shoulder. "Sure beats the tension and the arguing. We've always had fun together. I miss that. I miss us."

She missed *them*, too…so much she was aching inside.

"Me, too," she admitted.

He went to say something and then stopped, smiling instead. "Won't be long. I'll save you some water."

The rest of the morning had an odd tempo. Not their usual dynamic, but not the tightly strung, tense, almost borderline antagonism that had started seep-

ing into the cracks of their relationship. After breakfast and taking turns showering, they returned to the
Realtor's office and inspected two possible rental
properties. Winona fell in love with the second one,
a house on leafy Maple Street just out of town. It
was a large, Colonial Revival–style home, two-story,
with a fabulously accentuated front door, wide porch
with slender columns and windows with double-hung
sashes.

"This was an estate sale and so has been empty
for some time," the agent explained as they walked
around the house. "I'm sure it will go on the market
at some point, but the previous owner left it to her
stepson and he's happy for it to be a rental for the
moment. He lives in Yankton and has no interest in
residing in Cedar River."

Winona looked around some more, going from
room to room, seeing the beauty in the polished timber floors, hand-carved staircase and large stone fireplace in the living room. And the yard was huge with
an array of shrubs and flowers and a large chokecherry tree in one corner. She wandered around the
garden, spotting a bird feeder hanging from a tree
branch. It would be a lovely house to raise a family in.

"I love it," she said to Grant as the Realtor walked
back inside, giving them some privacy. "It's probably out of my price range, though."

He frowned. "What?"

"Well, I have no intention of dodging my share
of the rent."

He stopped walking and they both knew exactly what the conversation was about. "Are you going to be stubborn about everything?"

"No," she replied. "Just planning on paying my share."

He exhaled heavily. "It's my job to financially look after my wife and child."

"That's a little old-fashioned, don't you think? I have a job, Grant. I work and pay my bills, something I will continue to do."

He walked away, hands on hips, his shoulders tight. Winona remained where she was, watching him, feeling the tension between them grow as the seconds ticked by. Whenever he had something on his mind he always took a moment to reflect, to think, to consider his response. This was no different.

Finally, he turned, hands still on his lean hips. "Is everything going to be a battle? Can you at least meet me in the middle?"

"Of course," she replied. "The middle is me paying my share in everything."

"Look," he said, clearly exasperated. "I don't mean to come across old-fashioned, and I'll try harder to stop—I promise. But you and me and the baby are a family now. It's important to me to take care of my family. Despite you thinking I'm being bossy, I'm right here, doing this, *with* you. I'm honestly not trying to be demanding or last-century—just worthy of you both."

Winona stared at him, startled by the rawness of his admission, by the quiet intensity in his voice. And by the way his words made her feel. Feelings that suddenly had nowhere to go. Except into concession.

"Okay," she said softly, her heart banging so loudly behind her ribs she was sure he could hear it. "If you want to take care of the rent and the other things, then fine. But I will need to contribute something, understand? I have my pride and don't relish the idea of financially depending on anyone."

"I'm pretty sure we stopped being just *anyone* to one another a long time ago."

Of course he was right. And that was what made it so hard. If they were newly acquainted as well as being newly married, the situation would be very different. But they knew each other too well to negotiate.

"That's why it's so hard," she said, verbalizing her thoughts.

"Because we don't have any secrets from one another, you mean?"

I do have a secret...

And it twisted at her, churning her insides, making her mad with him but mostly with herself. Loving Grant had been her one constant for years. Being *in love* with him—silently acknowledging the resurgence of feelings she believed she'd tucked away forever—that made everything different between them. Because she was in love with him...had never stopped. She'd only buried her feelings away because she believed they were destined to be best friends forever. Not lovers.

And certainly not husband and wife.

"What if we bring more to this than we get back?" she asked, wondering if he'd read between the lines of her words—if he'd know she was talking about her loving him.

But he didn't. He was only ever about the facts. "Everything I own, every penny I have, I would give to you in a heartbeat," he said quietly. "Before Vegas, after Vegas. It's only money, Winnie. And since you've called me short-arms-long-pockets for years, I would think you'd like seeing me dip into the stash. I've never been much of a spender."

She laughed. She had called him that many times over the years. Oh, he was generous in nature, but had never been someone to splash out on frivolous things. He bought quality over quantity. Everything he owned was a considered purchase, made to last and be functional. She may have laughed about it at times, but the truth was, she admired his ability to save and be sensible. He owned his apartment and his car and she was sure he had a sizable bank balance.

"Should we get a prenup?" she asked quickly. "Or postnup in our case? You bring way more financial security to this marriage than I do."

"Didn't you hear what I just said?" he asked, his voice ominously low. "About giving you everything I have? I don't care about money, Winnie. If I have it, it's yours."

She knew that, because he was a lot of things—and honest was at the top of the list. She conceded a little more for the sake of harmony. "So—this house? Let's do it."

He sighed and she heard an almost palpable relief in the gesture. A few minutes later they were back inside and discussing the lease agreement with the Realtor.

"I'll call the owner today so we can process your application quickly," the Realtor said and looked at Grant. "I manage a couple of your brother's rental properties, so I'm sure I can provide the owner with a reference on your behalf," she said and grinned.

"How many houses does Joss own?" Winnie asked once they were back in the car and heading into town.

"A few, I think," he replied. "Joss has got quite the property portfolio and is giving the O'Sullivans a run for their money."

Everyone knew the rich O'Sullivan family owed a substantial portion of the commercial real estate in town. "Since Leah's going to marry one of them, we should learn to like them, I guess."

"Old habits," he said and grinned. "And Sean's okay—he's not as stuffy and entitled as some of them," he said of Leah's boyfriend.

Once they returned to the Realtor's office, they quickly filled out the relevant application forms and Winona was suddenly put on the spot when she was filling in the section with her name.

Winona Culhane...

Could she do it? As a teenager she'd doodled the words countless times. She'd dreamed it. Fantasized about it. Cried over it the day he announced he had his first girlfriend. Cursed herself over it time and time again when she knew it was a pipe dream.

He was sitting beside her, waiting for her to finish signing the form, and she could feel the heat from his gaze searing through her skin. She noticed her hand was shaking as she wrote and she took a steadying breath. Looking at her new signature—which was both familiar and crazily unbelievable—the reality of their situation pressed down on her shoulders. They were married. Having a baby. Setting up house together. She was living her secret dream. Winona should have been singing her happiness from the rooftops. She wasn't because it didn't feel real.

They were on the street, walking toward the bakery, when he spoke again. "There's something I'd like you to do."

"What?"

"Wear your wedding ring."

Winona almost tripped up. "Ah..."

"Or rather, wear *a* ring," he clarified. "Honestly, I'd like us to get new ones."

Winona glanced at the ring on his finger, noticing how bare her own seemed. "Why?"

"Because this ring was bought for someone else," he reminded her and tapped the wedding band he wore.

With her emotions already stretched, Winona wasn't sure she wanted a battle, but she didn't want to simply comply, either. "Seems like a waste of money when we have perfectly good rings."

"Is everything about money to you?"

It was an odd thing for him to say. He knew she had certain beliefs about things, and wasting money was one of them. She'd spent her early years with a mother who lived week-to-week mostly on welfare, and by the time she began living with Red on the ranch, she'd already got into the habit of being careful with her pennies. It wasn't about being frugal—it was about pride, and her need to work for what she had and pay her way. She knew he was generous, but not wasteful, and usually it was one of the things she admired about Grant—even if she did tease him every now and then. But he'd never been poor...and Winona knew what poor was firsthand. She knew hand-me-down clothes, food stamps and going hungry as a child. Grant had lived on the ranch all his life, enjoying the comforts of family money, and even when his mom died and Billie-Jack was left to run the place for a couple of years, Mitch and his aunt Sandra had ensured the place stayed afloat.

"I don't think money is everything," she said quietly. "But our childhoods were a little different."

"I know that, okay. And I'm certainly not trying to blow off your concerns about money," he said and grabbed her hand when she realized they were outside Cedar River's only jewelry store. "You're right, our lives were very different growing up. I know the struggles you experienced before you came to live with Red. But I'm asking you, please, can we do this?"

His gentle tone undid all of her resentment and she gave in with a hesitant smile. "Sure. Okay, let's go look."

Winona had been into the shop many times over the years to buy gifts for her grandfather and some of her friends. The fob watch she'd bought Grant for his twenty-first birthday came from the small but well-stocked store.

Deep down, she wanted to protest. To refuse the suggestion because it seem pointless. But something held her back.

This ring was bought for someone else...

It hadn't occurred to her that *he* might have any insecurities. Maybe it was just plain old macho conditioning. She couldn't be sure. And since Grant wasn't renowned for expressing his feelings, she was left with questions rather than the answers she longed for.

Grant wasn't quite sure why he was making such a big deal about the rings. But it had been niggling at him for days. Weeks even. Distracting him when he should have been thinking about a dozen other things. But the last couple of days had solidified his belief that they were doing the right thing by staying married and trying to make it work for their baby. Their child needed both parents. And he certainly didn't want to be a part-time father. He didn't do anything in half measures. He was all or nothing. In or out. Black or white. It was how he'd always lived his life.

And yeah, his relationship with Winnie was strained, intense and at times downright awkward, but they cared enough about one another to push past the hard stuff—he was sure of it.

He watched her move around the store, her fingers trailing across the edge of the cabinets as she perused the displays. He knew she liked sparkly things and watched her expression lift into a smile as she walked around. The jeweler, a middle-aged man who'd taken over the store from his father, attended to them immediately.

"How about that one?" Grant suggested, looking at a large oval-shaped solitaire diamond.

She joined him at the cabinet. "That's an engagement ring."

"It's usually the custom to have one."

"These are not usual circumstances."

He shrugged. "Maybe not, but the less attention we draw to the fact, the better, don't you think?"

She didn't look impressed by that remark, either.

While she perused the cabinet, Grant looked at the wedding bands, found one he liked and tried it on. It fit and he nodded agreeably.

"They're all so expensive," she said, almost to herself.

He knew that look—knew she was deep in thought, imagining the worst, thinking about how wasteful it all was. But Grant wasn't about to bend on the issue. And he wasn't prepared to question why. "Just pick one that you like."

"If you insist on a rock, I like this one," she said and pointed to a baguette emerald surrounded by diamonds.

He admired the stone and waited while she tried it on. It fit perfectly and the jeweler remarked how it was unusual to find an exact fit the first time.

"A wedding band, too," Grant said and gestured to a selection of bands in the cabinet.

She took only a few seconds to find one she liked and the jeweler passed it to Grant. "I think that's your department," he said.

Grant took the ring and grasped Winona's hand, waiting until the other man moved away from the counter before he spoke. "So," he said and slipped the ring on her finger. "For better or worse? For richer or poorer? To honor and cherish?" He lingered over the words for a moment. "We know how the rest goes, right?"

Her eyes glistened so brilliantly he had to fight the lump thickening his throat. "Yes, I think we do."

"Here," he said and held out the band he'd chosen. "Your turn."

She placed the ring on his finger, curling her hand in his. "Tell me we're doing the right thing."

Grant cupped her cheek. "We are. You and me," he reminded her. "We always do what's right. That's just who we are."

She inhaled deeply and smiled. "Okay."

Half an hour later, the rings selected and paid for and the paperwork completed, they left the store and headed to the bakery.

"They feel a little weird," she said and shook her left hand. "And ridiculously expensive. I'm glad you opted in for the insurance, because I'm terrified I'll lose them."

"They fit perfectly," Grant said and grabbed her hand, linking their fingers. "So the risk of losing them is small. Stop worrying. There's a pawn shop in Rapid City we can take the old ones to, if you like."

She shrugged, and when they reached the bottom of the stairway leading up to her apartment, she turned to face him. "Thank you," she said and stood on her toes and kissed his cheek.

He flushed with pleasure. "It's been quite a day, hasn't it? What do you say we go to JoJo's for pizza tonight?"

She agreed and they spent a companionable evening hanging out together.

But Grant knew she was faking it. He could feel it right through to his bones. Because he was faking it, too, so much that his jaw actually ached from the tight smile he forced himself into presenting every time she looked his way.

Back in the apartment by nine that evening, they went their separate ways at bedtime. He stayed up and did some prep work on his laptop for a job in Duluth the following week, while she headed for her bedroom. There was no late-night tea party, like there had been the night before. There was no repeat of the conversation about sex and definitely no kissing.

Which, as it turned out, was pretty much all he'd thought about for most of the day. Her perfume, for one thing, seemed to suddenly have a mind of its own and attacked his good sense at every opportunity, making him wonder about how much of the scent lingered on her skin by the end of the day. And her lips had been driving him crazy all afternoon—whether she was smiling, scowling or kissing his cheek. And her beautiful, sexy, memories-of-it-draped-over-his-chest hair wasn't doing his libido any favors, either.

The following day they headed to the ranch in the morning and endured Mitch, Tess and Ellie's scrutiny for a couple of hours. Hank was there for a visit and Grant dealt with a few minutes of query from his sensible, rock-solid brother while they were alone in the living room.

"Joss said last week you were getting a divorce?"

He nodded. "Things have changed. We're trying to work it out."

Hank chuckled. "Well, then, congratulations. You heading to Leah's tonight?"

"That was the plan," he replied.

"I'm on duty," Hank said. "I think Joss is going. The girls are with his in-laws this weekend and I think Leah is trying to set him up with the new museum curator."

"Well, you and Joss are the only single Culhanes left," Grant reminded him.

"And Ellie," Hank corrected.

"Don't kid yourself," Grant said and grinned. "She's half in love with Alvarez—she just won't admit it."

Hank's brows shot up. "I thought she despised him?"

"Same thing, really."

Hank laughed. "I guess. So, are you guys taking a honeymoon?"

He realized it wasn't something he and Winnie had talked about. "We haven't really discussed it. There's been a lot of other stuff going on."

"I suppose eloping and a baby on the way will do that," Hank remarked, still grinning. "I'm sure you'll be a good dad, though. Better than the one we had, that's for sure."

It was the perfect opening for Grant to mention Billie-Jack—but the words stuck in his throat for a few seconds. Of all the people their father's reckless-ness had impacted, Hank was the one who'd suffered the most. "Have you forgiven him?" he asked quietly, aware of the sudden stillness in the room.

Hank's expression flattened. "I try not to think about him."

"Yeah, me, too."

"You and Ellie were younger," Hank said evenly. "You needed him more. And the rest of us had Mom for longer and knew what a good parent was like."

"I miss her a lot," Grant admitted.

"Me, too," Hank said and sighed. "She had a way of making everything seem like it would work out. She was the glue that held us all together. Like Mitch is now. But, you know, forgiveness is a funny thing. It can creep up on a person over time. I don't hate Billie-Jack like I did. I don't wonder like I did. I guess I've put the memory of him from my mind. To me, that's better than hanging on to anger and resentment."

Grant admired his brother's resolve. But unlike Hank, he *was* curious about Billie-Jack. And maybe his brother was right—he'd been younger and more impressionable when their father bailed and didn't have the maturity back then to compartmentalize his feelings like his older siblings had been able to.

One thing he did know—he wasn't about to burden anyone else with the knowledge that Billie-Jack had resurfaced after so many years. At least, not yet.

"Everything okay?"

They were on their way to the dinner party late that afternoon when Winona asked him the question. They'd barely spoken since arriving at the ranch and she knew him well enough to pick up on his mood.

"Just thinking about things."

She nodded and touched his arm. "You've been quiet the last few hours. Second thoughts?"

"About us?" he queried. "Of course not. I was wondering if you wanted to take a honeymoon. We haven't really talked about it."

"It's not necessary," she replied. "Everything about us is unorthodox. And with moving into the new place and the baby and everything else, I'm really not up for anything more."

"Okay," he said and shrugged as he turned the vehicle onto the bridge and headed down to the river. "Just trying to tick all the boxes."

"Well, stop it, will you," she snapped. "I don't need to be placated with sparkly rings and vacations. I agreed to do this and we're doing it."

"The rings were for me," he said. "The thought of wearing a wedding band you picked out for *him* bugged the hell out of me."

Her mouth opened. "You sound jealous."

"Well, of course I'm freakin' jealous," he said irritably. "A month ago you were rushing off to marry the guy."

Silence screeched between them. He'd said too much, admitted too much.

They reached the driveway of Leah's home and headed down it. There were several vehicles parked outside the big house and he recognized Joss's pickup and Jake's SUV. He wasn't usually restless about the idea of socializing but was pleased a couple of his brothers would be there.

She got out of the car and Grant was struck by how lovely she looked in a pale blue dress and sandals. It was a warm evening and there was a radiant hue on her cheeks. Was she glowing? Had pregnancy amplified her beauty? The notion struck him deep in the gut, and he experienced an acute sense of stupid male pride somewhere in the region that probably belonged in a museum. He'd never considered himself an alpha guy—more millennial than his tough, cowboy brothers.

"What are you thinking?" she asked as she came around the car.

"Actually, I was thinking how beautiful you look," he replied and hooked his arm through her elbow. "But I don't want to be accused of placating or ticking any more boxes."

Her brows shot up. "Or being a jerk, right?"

"Because I told my wife she's beautiful? Seems like that's my job." He led her toward the house. "Remember, I am new to the husband gig. Although forgiveness isn't something you're usually good at, try to overlook my rookie mistakes, will you."

She pulled her arm away as they reached the stairs. "Are you looking for an argument?" she asked.

"Maybe," he said and shrugged. "At least we're talking."

Her gaze was filled with unrelenting scrutiny. "What's gotten into you?"

His hair-trigger temper—something he usually kept under tight control—snapped. "I don't know. Maybe I'm tired of you looking for fault in everything I do."

Her skin visibly paled. "I don't do that."

"Sure you do," he shot back. "It's your *thing*, finding fault. Maybe if you'd found fault with your marine and realized he wasn't the one for you, we wouldn't be in this mess!"

The moment he said, he regretted it. Because Grant knew he sounded like a petulant, immature jerk. But he couldn't keep a plug on the thoughts— the *feelings*—churning through his system. It had been building for days, torturing him every now and then, threatening to break free and make him face exactly what he was—jealous. The bloodcurdling, stomach-dropping kind. He'd admitted it to her earlier in an off-the-cuff way, but since buying the rings he'd had hours to dwell, hours to consider his reasoning, hours to build a wall of defense around what he wasn't prepared to face.

He was jealous of the man she had been going to marry.

The man she had loved. Still loved, he suspected, because feelings didn't simply switch off, did they? And since he'd never been jealous before, the knowledge shocked Grant to his deepest core. It didn't make sense. She'd dated in the past, had a boyfriend—hell, she'd been seeing the marine for eighteen months—and not once in that time had he faced the feelings suddenly tormenting him. And now, out of the blue, he was filled with a black, relentless rage that he couldn't shift, couldn't quell and couldn't understand.

Her eyes darkened for a moment and he suspected she wanted to tell him to go straight to hell. But she didn't. Because the door opened and his cousin

Leah appeared. She greeted them both with a smile and a hug, making a cheerful comment about their marriage that fell flat between them as they headed inside.

But the tension remained. And Grant knew they were heading for a major confrontation.

The truth was, he didn't know how he was going to stop imagining that she wished she was married to someone else.

Chapter Nine

Winona had seen many of Grant's moods over the years. But never this one. He spent the evening skulking like a caged animal, restless, on edge, as though he was looking for an escape the whole time they were there.

She'd always believed she knew everything about him, but this was new—this was unlike anything she'd experienced before. He'd always been so indifferent in relationships, so casual, she'd never had reason to think he was capable of, well...jealousy.

But clearly he was. He'd said as much. For whatever reason.

She tried to ignore him as much as she could, but it was impossible. Dinner was informal, more like a barbecue, and she was able to mingle, to show off her sparkly rings, to talk about the unexpected turn of events to friends and laugh and smile and act as though nothing was amiss. But she felt the friction building between them and every time she met his gaze it was filled with words unsaid.

It was weird seeing so many Culhanes and O'Sullivans in the same place, but since Leah and Sean had hooked up, the dynamic between the two families had changed. She hung around Jake and his wife, Abby, for a while, answering questions about their rushed marriage, and smiled appropriately when her sister-in-law said how it was all so romantic.

But it wasn't.

A mess.

That's what he'd called it.

And it was pretty close to the mark. Like they were playacting at being married.

Faking it.

God, what am I doing...?

It had only been a few days and already the tension between them was unbearable. What would happen when they were really living together? How could they possibly make it work? Would they have separate bedrooms? The Maple Street house had three bedrooms and a study—plenty of room for them to sleep apart *and* have a place for the baby.

She looked around and spotted Leah by the buffet table, chatting to Joss and Jake. She and Leah and Ellie had always been the firmest of friends, and even though the other two women were cousins, they'd never left her out of their circle. She cared about both women deeply and felt ashamed that she'd pulled away from their friendship in the past month or so. Perhaps if she hadn't rushed off to Vegas and asked only Grant to be there, if she'd included them, then her life wouldn't now be so upside down. They would have consoled her when Dwight proved to be a no-show. They would have drunk margaritas together, cried a little, called him a few names and then returned home.

But there would be no baby...

And that was the kicker.

Because, despite everything, despite the fact she was deeply conflicted about her awkward relationship with Grant, she was over the moon about the prospect of having a baby. She'd always wanted a family of her own and couldn't stop the joy she felt every time she thought about the child she carried.

"So," Leah said as she sidled up beside her. "You're one for surprises."

Winona smiled. "Yeah...what can I say."

Leah was an artist, and with her long dark hair streaked with colors of pink and purple and in the flowing halter-style dress she wore, she looked unconventional. In her sensible blue outfit, Winona felt very ordinary beside her friend.

"Oh, I don't know," Leah said and smiled. "This

kind of thing usually has a way of working itself out. It's kind of romantic when you think about it."

"That's probably a stretch, since we got drunk and ended up in bed together," Winona said and then felt bad. She didn't want anyone speculating about her relationship with Grant. "Well, anyway, we're trying to work it out as we go."

"That's all any of us can do," her friend said and placed a comforting arm around her shoulders. "And don't be a stranger, okay?"

Winona nodded. "I'll try harder."

Leah's expression softened. "You know, you've always been family to me and Ellie, and now that you're married to Grant, you really are family. So, don't take this the wrong way, but we never believed Dwight was the right guy for you."

"You didn't?"

"No," her friend replied. "And I'm pretty sure you didn't, either. Do you remember that time we played Truth or Dare and you lost and I got to read a page out of your diary? I was about fifteen, you were fourteen?"

Memory rushed through her. She recalled the small, sparkly purple diary, the little notebook that held all her secrets. She still had it, tucked away in the back of the cupboard in her old bedroom at the ranch. "Yeah."

"Well, the page I read included these words, and I quote—'I want to marry him one day.' And I know you weren't talking about the latest pop star on MTV."

"Just teenage angst," Winona said, swallowing her embarrassment, recalling exactly the day and the moment she wrote the words about Grant in her diary. He was a senior in high school and was taking Missy Benson to prom, and Winona had cried on and off for days leading up to the event, knowing he'd be kissing Missy at the end of the evening, and maybe more. Also knowing that besides the soul-crushing fact they were friends, she was way too young for him back then. "It didn't mean anything."

"Maybe it does. Maybe it means everything worked out just as it was meant to. You know, it looks to me like you got what you asked for."

Winona stared at her friend, too stunned to speak. Because Leah was right. She did have what she'd wished for—all of it. Grant and a baby of her own. Maybe the way they came about wasn't exactly the stuff of fairy tales, but she had it all, nonetheless.

She looked across the room and spotted him near the wide door that opened onto the deck and he met her gaze instantly. She offered a tiny smile and he frowned, like he wasn't expecting a kind gesture, and it made her suck in a sharp breath.

I'm tired of you looking for fault in everything I do...

Was that really what she did? To everyone? Or to him alone?

She couldn't decide which option was the worst.

Either way, she experienced a deep surge of shame that ripped through her like a tornado.

It took her a few minutes to summon the courage to walk over to him. He was talking to Joss and she moved up beside him, saying nothing. She simply grasped his hand and linked their fingers, feeling him stiffen. But after a couple of seconds, he relaxed a little and his fingers tightened around hers.

"You okay?" he asked quietly when there was a break in the conversation.

Winona moved closer to him and spoke so only he could hear. "Can you take me home?"

His brow furrowed. "Something wrong?"

"No," she replied. "Just tired."

He was still frowning, but he nodded, and ten minutes later they were heading back into town. Winona didn't say much, just a passing comment about how nice the evening had been and how happy Leah seemed. He didn't respond, didn't say anything, really, merely a sort of half grunt that was acknowledgment of her words.

Back at the apartment, she walked on ahead and dropped her tote on the hall table near the door. She looked at him, noticing that he was now standing by the window, staring out to the street.

"Grant?"

He turned. "Yeah...good night."

Winona swallowed hard, finding courage from deep down, knowing they were somehow at a crossroads. She wasn't sure how they got there. But she knew she had to do something to save what they had, even if she didn't know what that was—or she suspected they were doomed.

"I don't mean to find fault in you," she said quietly.

He held up a hand vaguely. "I'm really not up for another argument."

"Me, either. Actually," she said and moved forward a few steps, taking a breath, "I was hoping that you might…"

"Might what?" he asked when her words trailed off.

She took another step. "Well, that you might want to forgo the couch tonight," she said, coloring hotly. "I mean, it can't be comfortable and there's really no reason why we shouldn't sleep in the same bed. We are married, after all."

One brow cocked at a sharp angle. "Huh?"

A little frustration set in. "I'm asking if you want to sleep with me tonight."

He took a moment, like he was deciding something difficult. "Isn't that against your ground rules?"

"We both know it was a dumb rule," she said and shrugged. "But suit yourself. I'm going to have a shower and go to bed."

She did what she said she would, racing through a shower, slathering on body lotion, slipping into a shell-pink satin nightgown, and was back in the bedroom brushing her hair when she heard the shower going again. She flicked on the bedside lamps, switched off the main light, and she was just rubbing on hand cream when he appeared in the doorway, silhouetted by the light behind, dressed in a white tank shirt and a pair of cotton boxers, one shoulder leaning against the jamb.

Her breath caught in her throat, and for a moment she was mesmerized by the image, catapulted back to those hours in Vegas when they had found passion in each other's arms. She wanted that again. Longed for it. Needed it like she needed air in her lungs.

"You know, Winnie," he said, his gaze slowly traveling over her. "If what you really want is for me to make love to you, you only have to ask."

She placed the brush on the dresser and straightened, sensing that they were in one of those pivotal moments. A moment there was no going back from. Only forward. Leah was right—she did have everything she ever wanted. And he'd tried, she knew, to make things as normal as possible. She knew it was up to her to reach out, to make a move, to set the rhythm of their relationship. To fix things, really, so they could have some kind of normal marriage. One that included intimacy.

She inhaled, finding strength from even deeper down than before. "Okay... I'm asking. Would you make love to me tonight?"

"Yes," he said and pushed himself off the jamb. "But I'd like you to answer a question first."

Her nerves rattled. "Sure."

"Why?" he asked. "What's changed?"

"Nothing," she replied, not really lying, because nothing had essentially changed. She'd simply gained some clarity and perspective about their relationship. About her role in their marriage and what she wanted. "I think I just needed some time, you know, to get things straight in my head. To adjust. Let's face it, the last month or so has been kind of overwhelming."

He nodded a little. "You're right, it's been surprising and...confusing."

"But I'm not confused about what I want," she said and took a few steps across the room, her toes digging into the carpet pile.

He met her by the bed, his gaze taking a leisurely trip down her body and back up as he stripped off his tank shirt and tossed it on the floor. She stared at his chest, his shoulders, his flat belly, the lines and contours of a physique that was perfectly proportioned and wholly masculine. She'd never tire of looking at him. Never find any other man as attractive, really, she realized as though she was suddenly in a kind of sexy dream with him in the starring role. Of course, he'd always played center stage in her dreams. Nothing had changed over the years. Only now, he was her husband and she could make her dreams a reality.

"So," he said softly, his voice deep and incredibly sexy. "What do you want?"

"You," she admitted, heat coursing through her veins. "This."

He smiled a little. "You wearing anything under that?" he asked, reaching out to touch her face.

"Not a thing," she replied, watching the pulse in his cheek.

His mouth was on hers within seconds and the kiss was hot, fierce and erotic. Winona wrapped her arms around him, touching his strong back, pushing herself closer, harder, tighter, wanting to feel all of him against her. He moaned low in his throat, deepening the kiss, taking her on a wild ride as their tongues met and withdrew over and over. His hands were in her hair, on her shoulders, on her hips, rubbing the silky fabric against her skin. When he cupped her behind and drew her hard against him, Winona was left with no doubt of his arousal. Any insecurities she had about his desire or attraction for her were abruptly sent offstage.

He sat on the bed and gently pulled her toward him, still kissing her, still tracing his fingertips across her skin in an erotic pattern. She sighed against his mouth, finding his tongue again and dueling with it, feeling a hot rush of need pool down low. She'd longed for passion like this, yearned for it. Dreamed of it. When he eased her back, she went willingly, her fingers threading through his hair as he kissed her mouth, her cheek, her neck, trailing downward to her throat. He pushed the nightgown straps down and trailed his mouth along her rib cage, finding her breasts and the nipples that ached for his caress. He circled one bud with his tongue, then the other, and she arched her back off the bed, experiencing pleasure so intense she could barely draw in a breath. She said his name, holding his head against her, urging him to continue the exquisite torture.

"Holy hell," he whispered raggedly against her flesh and swiftly dispensed with her nightgown, openly admiring her. "You're so beautiful, Winnie," he said as one hand dipped between her thighs and he caressed her intimately.

She wasn't sure how long they touched for—minutes, hours, eternity. But she came apart, once, twice, feeling as though she was flying as the pleasure overwhelmed her senses. Then all she knew was that she needed to feel him, to run her fingers across his flesh and touch every part of him. She pressed her hands against his chest, feeling the muscles bunch, taking her own erotic journey across skin and sinew. She tugged at his boxers, dragging them over his hips, and reveled in the sheer beauty of his flesh.

Oddly, there was nothing shy or reserved about the way they made love. It wasn't awkward. It wasn't forced. It was hot, heady and arousing, like it had been in Vegas. He gave, she gave, he led and then she followed. But she took, too, touching him with her hands and mouth and with a confidence she hadn't known she possessed. He did that, she thought as pleasure overtook them, he taught her to take what she wanted, what she needed.

And finally, when they could take no more and craved release, he moved over her, resting his weight on his elbows, his green eyes never leaving hers as they joined together. She matched every move, every kiss, every thrust and erotic slide, and as the pressure built, so did the love that she felt through to the depths of her soul. She tumbled headlong into a vortex of pleasure so intense she couldn't get enough air in her lungs, holding him, grasping at him, as he tumbled with her in a white-hot rush of release.

Afterward, he rolled off her gently, grasping her hand and raising it to his lips. "Are you okay?" he asked, his voice low and raspy.

"Perfect," she said on a sigh.

"Yes," he said and exhaled, "you certainly are."

Grant knew that sex could addle a man's brain. Great sex, however, also did something else. It made him crave. Like he'd never quite craved before. In the past, sex was something enjoyable he did with someone he liked. Afterward, though, he would swiftly forget about the intimate connection and get on with his life.

But he didn't simply like Winnie. He loved her. And that changed sex.

The thing was, up until two hours ago, he hadn't quite believed that to be true.

But now, as he lay beside his wife, her lovely arm draped across his belly, her hair fanned over his chest, he was struck by how content and *happy* he was. The scent of her assailed him, reaching him on some sensory level he was unfamiliar with. Normally, after sex, he'd be asleep within twenty minutes, but for reasons he couldn't define, he didn't want to miss one moment of watching her, feeling her, experiencing her.

And it shocked him deeply.

She moved, moaning softly, and he soothed her with a gentle rocking motion. She was so beautiful, so uninhibited, so naturally sensual, that their lovemaking had taken him to another place. Another dimension. He felt ridiculous thinking it, but he couldn't dismiss the notion.

He kissed her forehead and she sighed, rolling a little, linking one of her legs around his. He could feel her belly pressed against his thigh, and wondered how long it would be before her pregnancy started showing. He wanted her to show, he wanted to splay his hand across her stomach and feel their child moving beneath his palm. The idea filled him with an excitement that he couldn't fathom. He'd never believed he was one of those people who felt deeply, too afraid of letting his guard down to allow anyone to get inside, but Winnie was well and truly in deep. So was their baby.

And somehow, instead of the normal anxiety he experienced thinking about it, as he lay with her in his arms, his pulse rate slowly winding down after such an intense physical release, Grant experienced an incredible sense of calm.

He slept, waking up around dawn to the lovely sensation of her hands stroking his chest. She lay on her side, the sheet tangled at their feet, her eyes closed, her fingertips touching him in a way that was both erotic and hypnotic.

"You keep doing that and I'm never going to get out of this bed," he said and grasped her hand, bringing her knuckles to his mouth and kissing her softly.

She didn't open her eyes. But she smiled. "That's my plan, Culhane," she whispered. "Although I can think of some other things I could also do."

Grant chuckled. "Be my guest."

Her eyes sprang open and she looked at him, all sexy and wanton and so hot he felt awareness creep back into his limbs and then move higher, because he was completely at her mercy. She didn't need another invitation and quickly moved over him, lying breast to chest, hip to hip, thigh to thigh, her hair cascading like a waterfall around them.

Within seconds he was inside her, and she straddled him, rising to her knees, gripping his hands and moving her hips in a way that almost sent him directly over the edge into that place that was a mix of both heaven and hell. She didn't speak, didn't do anything other than rotate her hips, creating an aching hunger in his blood that defied belief. When release came it was swift, sharp and soul-deep. He watched her through a daze of pleasure, feeling closer to her in that moment than he had ever felt to anyone else, ever.

She collapsed against him, breathing hard, her breasts pressed to his chest, her mouth quickly finding his in a kiss that was filled with passion and heat. He could barely breathe, but still kissed her, still took her tongue into his mouth, still gripped her hips to maintain the intensely intimate connection of their bodies.

"Now I'm definitely not getting out of this bed," he said on a strangled breath.

She laughed and the lovely sound reverberated in his chest. "Not even for your morning run?"

His brows shot up. "Seriously, do you think I have any energy left for running?"

She laughed again. "Dig deep, husband."

He liked the way she said the word and experienced a foolish sense of companionship and pride in that moment. He chuckled and rolled them both in one gentle movement, half pinning her beneath him. "Although, I gotta say, this isn't the most comfortable mattress in the world. We should go furniture shopping as soon as we know if we got the house."

"You're not planning on bringing your furniture from your apartment?" she asked, a little more seriously.

"Nah... I don't think all that chrome and glass would look any good in the Maple Street house. And I think we should get new stuff, you know, for a new start."

"Let's do the shopping together, as long as we split the bill," she said, clearly looking for a compromise. "It'll be fun. I can't wait to start buying baby things."

The look in her eyes when she spoke about the

baby created an ache deep in his chest. "You're really happy about the baby, aren't you?" he asked, seeing pure joy in her expression.

She nodded. "I've always wanted kids, you know that. I guess it's because I had such a dysfunctional time growing up, before I moved in with Papa. And then I met you and saw what a real family was like. I want that for our children, Grant."

"Children?"

Her eyes shuttered for a moment. "I'd always planned to have two or three if I could."

"I guess I'm still reeling from the idea of one," he said, teasing her a little, "but I'll come around. Besides," he said and trailed a kiss from her ear to her mouth. "Making them is fun."

They stayed in bed for another half an hour, kissing, touching, talking about silly things. When he hauled himself up she seemed shy, covering herself with a duvet for a moment, and then she shrugged and dropped the cover, walking across the room naked before slipping into a cotton robe.

"Bit late for modesty, right?" she said.

"A little," he replied. "What would you like to do today?"

She glanced at the bed. "I'm sure we'll think of something."

They headed out to O'Sullivan's for breakfast a little later, and when they returned to her apartment, Grant did some work for a couple of hours. She interrupted him every now and then, offering coffee or a snack, sometimes more, which was incredibly tempting and distracting. It was far removed from the tense, almost distant dynamic of the previous days and he liked it...a lot.

"You know," he said and grabbed her hand when she walked past the small table where he was working, and gently pulled her onto his lap. "The more you distract me, the longer this is going to take and the less time I'll have to make love to you tonight."

"I know," she said and curled her arms around his neck, dipping her head to kiss his throat. "But I can't help myself. I wish you didn't have to leave tomorrow."

"Me, too," he said and rested his hands on her hips. "But I have some prep work I need to do and my flight for Duluth leaves early on Tuesday morning."

"When will you be back?" she said, kissing the spot just below his earlobe and making him crazy.

"Thursday," he replied raggedly. "Friday morning at the latest."

She pressed closer, distracting him even more. "How many of you are going?"

"Three," he replied. "Bill from tech support, Krystal and myself."

She pulled back immediately. "Krystal?"

"She's the training leader for this project," he said and saw the hesitation in her eyes. "Don't stress, she knows I'm married now."

"I'm not stressed. How'd she take it?"

"You know, I didn't wait around to ask. But I'm pretty sure she couldn't care less."

"What makes you so sure?"

"Because she's dating Bill from tech support," he said and grinned. "What are you planning on doing this week?" he asked, trying to shift his thoughts from X-rated to a more appropriate G-rated, and figured he'd have to settle on M-rated because she kept kissing his neck and it was mind-blowing.

"Start packing, I guess. And I need to talk to Regina about breaking my lease."

He nodded agreeably. "Have you given any more thought to her offer, you know, to go into a partnership?"

She sighed against his skin. "Yes. I need to think about my future. I need to do something with my life."

"You can do anything you want," he said, stroking her hips in a way that spiked his libido up another notch. "You're smart, beautiful, funny—"

"Broke," she reminded him.

"You know," he said as he grasped her chin and tilted her face to meet his, "we could go into the venture together. What's mine is yours, remember?"

Her brown eyes were warm and slumberous, filled with a kind of glazed desire that reached him deep down. "Together?"

"Business partners as well as husband and wife."

He hoped she'd make some concession and was pleased when she did.

"Okay, I'll think about it."

"Thank you," he said and kissed her softly.

"For what?"

"Not immediately putting a wall up," he replied. "For considering it. I heard the trick to a good marriage is compromise."

Her brows rose. "Did you just make that up?"

"Maybe," he conceded. "But it sounds about right. By the way, I'm gonna miss you this week."

She smiled, kissing him. "Me, too. Poor Krystal," she said, still smiling. "Doesn't know what she's missing."

He kissed her hotly and got to his feet, quickly forgetting about work, and carried her down the hall and into the bedroom. They made love in a leisurely way, ignoring the fact it was still light outside and that the lazy Sunday afternoon was doing its thing on the street below. Grant knew he'd never get enough of the taste of her lips, or the scent of her skin, or the touch of her hands.

And it floored him.

Of course he'd experienced desire before, and in varying degrees, but never with the burning intensity he felt for Winnie. The more he touched her, the more he wanted her. The more she gave, the more he wanted to give. It was jarring to his usual self-control. Because there was nothing controlled about the feelings coursing through him—feelings that were shifting and changing at an alarming rate.

No, he corrected, not changing…that wasn't it.

They were doing something else—they were intensifying. As though they'd lain dormant since eternity and were suddenly allowed to come to life. Now, he wondered how he'd even gotten through a day without kissing her, without thinking of her as more than just his friend.

Because this wasn't simple friendship, he thought as they held one another. It was deeper and more real than anything he'd experienced before.

It was high stakes.

And he realized, maybe for the first time in his life, what he had to lose.

Everything.

Chapter Ten

They got the house on Maple Street, which was just as well because Winona had already started packing up her apartment. Grant called her Wednesday from Duluth and said the Realtor had contacted him that afternoon and would call her the following day to make arrangements for the key collection and some further documents to sign.

She was excited but couldn't quell the uneasiness that crept up on her every now and then. She couldn't quite define it. It wasn't overt. It wasn't grounded in anything substantial. They needed a bigger place, end of story. But still, she was rattled. She didn't say anything to Grant because she knew he would either dismiss her reservations—if that's even what they were—or placate her with assurances that they were doing the right thing. And yes, she agreed...mostly.

She'd believed, or at least hoped, that physical intimacy would bring them closer. But deep down she felt that being lovers had created an even wider divide. The sex was wonderful, and in his arms, she experienced pleasure and tenderness she hadn't known existed. But in her heart she knew it hadn't brought them closer—it only amplified how far apart they really were.

And made her lonelier than she ever imagined she could feel.

She longed to talk to him about it, but the words wouldn't come.

Winona worked morning shifts that week, and on Thursday she stopped by the ranch to see her grandfather. Of course, she spoke to him every day on the phone, but that wasn't the same as having a real visit.

She spotted Ellie hanging by the corral and figured as well as visiting Red she had some ground to make up with her friend. They'd hardly spoken in the past month or so, and Winona missed their friendship.

"Hey," she said when she approached. "You didn't make it to Leah's last Saturday night?"

Ellie pointed to the mare and young foal at foot that were prancing around the corral. "I was on foal watch," she explained. "This mare had trouble foaling last time, so Mitch and I didn't want to leave her in case anything went wrong."

"He's beautiful."

Ellie nodded. "One thing I gotta say about Alva-rez—that champion stallion of his throws beautiful progeny. Speaking of which," Ellie said and glanced at her stomach. "How's my niece or nephew doing?"

Winona touched her belly. "Great. You know, we haven't had a chance to really talk about it."

Ellie shrugged. "What's to say. You married my brother and now you're having a baby. Once I got over the shock, I wasn't really surprised."

Winona suspected as much. In all the years they'd known one another, Ellie had never betrayed her. "You've never said anything…you know, about my feelings for Grant. To him, I mean. I know you've never come and asked, but I think you've always suspected."

"That you're madly in love with him?" Ellie said and grinned. "Of course I knew. I think the only per-son who was totally clueless was my brother. But he knows now and that's all that matters, right?"

She swallowed hard. Because he didn't know, did he? And how could she tell him when she knew he wouldn't say it in return. That would be devastating and humiliating. "Yeah, sure. We found a house— would you like to come by tomorrow and see it?"

"Love to," Ellie replied.

They made arrangements to meet up at Maple Street the following afternoon. "You can help me decorate."

Ellie smiled. "I'm really happy it all worked out for you both."

"Me, too," Winona said.

"You know what this means, don't you?" Ellie queried.

Winona's brows rose up. "What?"

"We're sisters now," her friend supplied. "Like we always wanted to be when we were kids."

Winona felt an incredible sense of inclusion and belonging in that moment, and quickly hugged her friend. She was still thinking about Ellie's words a little later when she was at the cottage with her grandfather sipping tea and talking about general things—the garden, the new chicken run he'd helped Mitch build. Then he changed the subject.

"How are things between you and Grant?"

"Ah...fine. Why?" she asked.

"Just making sure you're okay," he replied. "That's a grandfather's job."

"I'm fine," she insisted. "I promise. Papa, when we told you we were married and were having a baby, you didn't seem all that surprised."

"I wasn't," he said. "You and Grant go way back. I was probably surprised it hadn't happened sooner. But then you were dating that marine for a while."

Dwight? How long had it been since she'd even spared him a thought? As for thinking she was in love with him, just the notion made her twitch. So much of her life had changed in the past weeks.

"I never really loved Dwight."

"I know that," Red said. "I know you've been look-ing for love your whole life, Win. After your mother ran off and left you here, it left a little hole inside you, right?"

Emotion rose up and tightened her throat. "I sup-pose it did."

"Natural," he said gently, his eyes wrinkling at the corners. "And this old man wasn't much good at being both a mom and a dad."

"You were amazing," she assured him. "You still are. I've never been sorry Mom left me here, Papa. I know it was the best thing that could have hap-pened to me."

His eyes glistened. "She's not a bad person, you know. But she was always spirited when she was young. Then she got mixed up in the wrong crowd and started getting into trouble."

Winona had heard the story before. "She was young and everyone makes mistakes when they're young."

"Not you," Red said with a sudden smile. "You were an angel. And now you're married to that fine young man and have a baby coming. I couldn't be prouder."

"You like Grant, don't you?"

He nodded. "Always had a sensible head on his shoulders, even as a little kid. He'll be a good hus-band and father."

"I know he will," she said, her chest tightening. "I love him very much."

Red nodded approvingly. "He loves you, too. I can see it when you're together."

Winona wanted to believe, wanted to imagine that the feelings he felt for her were more than friendship, more than duty for the child they had made. But self-preservation warned her that wishes were for romantic fools. And romantic fools inevitably ended up with a broken heart. Which was why, when he didn't return to Cedar River on Friday, like he'd promised he would, Winona was imagining all kinds of things.

The truth was, since they'd had such an incredible time together the previous weekend, she'd anticipated that he couldn't wait to get home quick enough—that he was as hungry for her as she was for him. When all she could do was think about being in his arms and feeling his hands all over her, it was clearly not the case for her husband. Sure, when he called Thursday evening and said he was delayed and wouldn't be home until Saturday, she longed to ask him what was so important. She knew he was committed to his work, but irrationally she expected him to put everything aside so he could keep his word. She wanted to start nesting and planning, not sit around pining because he was in another state. She knew she'd sounded tense on the call, and although he said he missed her, she longed for more. She wanted to say she loved him, like they used to do, before their relationship took a dive into something so complicated she didn't even have the words to describe it. She wanted him to reply with his usual *Ditto*. She wanted something. *Anything.* Just some assurance that she wasn't the greatest lovesick fool of all time.

Grant couldn't remember the last time he'd been so nervous. Maybe never. Maybe it wasn't really nerves. Perhaps it was plain and simple dread.

I'm seeing my father for the first time in eighteen years.

He wasn't sure what he expected. What he wanted. And over the past twenty-four hours he'd changed his mind about seeing Billie-Jack half a dozen times.

But now, here he was—sitting opposite the man who he hated and despite everything, still loved— and kept wondering what the hell he was doing.

Billie-Jack. Cancer. Chemo.

The three things were now etched in his brain. After weeks of avoiding it, Grant finally picked up when his father had called again and after several tense minutes, agreed to meet him.

For coffee, he'd first thought, and made arrangements to meet him at a café in Rapid City. Those first few minutes had been unbearably tense. There was no handshake, no hug, just an acknowledging nod. It also took Grant about thirty seconds to figure out that the old man was sick. Billie-Jack looked frail and like a shadow of the person he remembered.

"Yeah, the cancer's got me," his father said, clearly picking up on his observations. "I've been getting treatment. My doctor has arranged for me to continue at the hospital here."

Grant didn't know what to think…or feel. "Why did you call me?"

His father shrugged his bony shoulders. "I wanted to see you…to talk."

Grant's gut rolled over. "About what? The past? Your illness? Redemption?"

"Just to talk," his father said again. "I ain't expecting a miracle."

"Good," Grant replied. "Because I'm all out."

Billie-Jack cracked a smile and then motioned to Grant's left hand. "You're married?"

He nodded. "I didn't agree to come here today to talk about my life."

"Fair enough," his father said. "How are your brothers? Your sister?"

"I didn't agree to come here today to talk about them, either. What is it you want, Billie-Jack?"

He couldn't call him Dad—the word just wouldn't come. All he really wanted to do was bail. He wanted to get back to his real life—the one that was now centered around Winnie and the baby they had coming. The one that had nothing to do with Billie-Jack. All he could think about was how unhappy she'd sounded when they'd spoken on the phone. And how all he wanted was to take her into his arms and reassure her that everything would be okay. That *they* would be okay.

"I want to make amends, if I can."

Amends? That meant forgiveness. It was too much to ask. Too much to give.

"I can't do this," he said and got to his feet. "I have to go."

"Grant, please," Billie-Jack said and grasped his forearm. "I know this is hard. I know you're angry and you have every right to be—but I just want to spend some time with you…while I have time left."

Grant's insides tightened. He wasn't usually someone who ran from hard things—but he had so much going on in his life, he didn't know if he had the time or patience for anything else. But as he looked down at his father, he saw real regret in the other man's expression, and it twisted at something deep inside.

"I'll call you later," he said. "We'll talk some more."

Then he left the café as quickly as he could.

Friday morning, after a night of restless dreams, Winona headed to the new house and made a list of all the things they needed to purchase. The house was mostly clean but had been empty for some time and needed a good airing and the banisters needed a polish. She stopped by the hardware store and picked up some supplies after lunch and was unloading the parcels when Ellie arrived.

Her friend was dressed in jeans and an old shirt. "I'm here to help."

They spent the next few hours cleaning and laughing and reminiscing about their teenage years. Ellie ducked out to get coffee and donuts around three thirty and while she was gone Winona experienced a wrenching sense of melancholy. Sadness even. It should have been the happiest time of her life. She was hanging out with a friend and preparing rooms that would soon be filled with her own family. But all she felt was lost and alone.

"Win?" Ellie's voice cut through her thoughts. "Are you all right?"

She wiped her eyes, mortified that she was now crying, and continued hanging the living room curtains she'd ordered online. They were a little wrinkled, but Ellie assured her the creases would fall out quickly.

"I'm fine," she lied.

"You're upset?" her friend said and came across the room.

She shook her head. "Oh, this is my new thing… crying," she added and gave a self-deprecating laugh. "I'm sure it's just pregnancy hormones running riot."

Ellie draped an arm across her shoulders. "Are you sure? Is something bothering you? Is everything okay?"

She sucked in a breath and nodded, trying to ease the ache in her chest. "I don't know why I'm teary and emotional."

"Well, you've had a lot of change in your life recently, and that's a big upheaval."

"Is it?" she challenged, her voice higher than usual as she moved away, wrapped her arms around her waist and then turned to face her friend. "It shouldn't be. Because I have everything I ever wanted. I mean,

I'm married to your brother and I'm having his baby and we're just about to move into this great house and I should be jumping up and down with happiness."

"But you're not, is that what you're saying?"

The emotions she'd been holding back for the past few weeks suddenly rushed to the surface and she couldn't stop the fresh tears that burned her eyes. Ellie was her friend, one of the best she'd ever had. But she was also Grant's sister and that meant loyalties could be strained. She certainly didn't want to cause any stress between the siblings, but in that moment, she needed a friend.

"I can't quite explain what I'm feeling... I'm confused," she admitted. "It's like I have this shadow hovering over me, and I hurt whenever I think about it."

"I'm not sure I understand," Ellie said, looking fraught. "Is this about my brother? Is your marriage in trouble?"

"I don't know," Winona said and sucked in a ragged breath. "You know how important you and your family are to me, right?"

"Of course. We care about you, too."

She nodded. "Grant and I have always had a strong friendship. Unbreakable. Unbendable. But now..."

"And now you don't, is that what you're saying?" Ellie frowned a little. "Even though you're married and—"

"It doesn't make sense, does it?" she said and sighed. "I know that. But I miss what we *had*. I miss

the way things used to be, how *we* used to be, when
we were just friends. How we would talk and laugh
and confide in one another. We don't do that like we
used to—we don't connect like we did before all this
happened." The words tumbled out, each one hurting
more than the last, and she took a moment to regather
her composure, wiping the tears off her cheeks.

"Maybe you guys need to talk more," Ellie suggested. "Take a trip, spend some alone time together,
have a honeymoon. A real one."

She shrugged. "Grant actually suggested it...but I
thought we had too much going on—you know, trying to settle into a new situation—to add something
else to the mix."

"Tell him you've changed your mind," Ellie said.
"He'd go along with it in a heartbeat."

It sounded like a nice idea, Winona thought as
she went back to the window and fluffed out the
curtains. And she was certain Grant would take her
wherever she wanted to go. But a honeymoon vaca-
tion wasn't the cure for what ailed their relationship.
That was the truth. And she wasn't sure she had the
courage to face it.

She took a few long breaths and glanced at her
friend. "Everything changed so fast and I...I miss
him," she admitted. "I miss him *so* much."

"What are you going to do?" Ellie asked caringly.
"Are you going to tell Grant how you feel?"

"I don't know. I know I can't go back. I know I
have a baby on the way and I have to live my life in

the present. But I feel…" Her voice trailed off for a moment and she struggled for the word. "Heartbroken."

She heard something, like footsteps, and was stunned to suddenly see Grant framed in the doorway. He wore suit pants and a blue shirt, sans the tie, like he'd come straight from the office. And he looked tired, she noticed.

She blinked and hoped the tears were gone from her eyes. "Hi," she said quickly. "What are you doing here? I thought you weren't coming back until tomorrow."

"I managed to change things around," he replied and moved into the room as he looked toward Ellie. "Hey, Brat."

"Hi," Ellie said as her gaze darted back and forth between them both. "It's good to see you. Well, I should probably get going. It's been fun hanging out," she said and quickly grabbed her bag. "Let me know if you guys need help moving."

She hugged them both and left.

Winona stayed where she was and stared at him, taking in his tight-shouldered stance and five-o'clock shadow. "I'm surprised to see you."

"Clearly," he replied tersely.

Winona shook herself off, walked across the room and kissed his cheek, inhaling the familiar scent of his cologne, which wrapped around her like a cloak. "Surprised, but glad. How did you know I'd be here?"

"I didn't," he said. "I went to your apartment first.

I bought you flowers, but they're also at the apartment."

"Flowers?"

He walked away, strolling around the room. "I thought it might cheer you up. Anyway, the place looks good. You should go furniture shopping in the morning."

She frowned. "Won't you be coming with me?"

"I have to get back to Rapid City in the morning for an appointment. I'll drive back in the afternoon if it's not too late."

Winona was confused. "So why did you come back today if you—"

"I came back for you."

Grant didn't know what to think…or what to make of what he had overheard, and his skin was burning so hot he could barely stand still. She missed her ex—is that what she was saying? She missed him and she was heartbroken.

"For me?"

He turned and looked at her. "You sounded unhappy on the phone last night. I thought perhaps I was needed here more than at…more than anywhere else."

More than seeing my father again…

But he didn't say that. Didn't want to burden her with the truth. He was still reeling from having met with Billie-Jack the day before, still couldn't get the image out of his head of the thin, sickly looking man who barely resembled the father he'd once known.

And he clearly wanted to make amends. He wanted so much. And all Grant wanted to do was see Winnie.

Now he almost wished he'd stayed in Rapid City.

Anything was better than hearing she was heartbroken over another man.

He'd missed her so much over the last few days. He'd longed to see her, feel her, have her in his arms. He was feeling so many conflicting emotions. Desire, resentment, anger—all of it directed at the one person he'd always held closest to his heart. That was the killer—that she didn't know. Didn't see. *Couldn't see.* For days—no, weeks—he'd been walking around in a daze trying to figure out what he was feeling, why he felt different, why every part of him ached, even his skin.

"How was Duluth?"

He shrugged. "Just another job."

"And Krystal?" she asked, surprising him.

Grant scowled. "What? Since when have you been so paranoid about Krystal? Seriously? Give me a break, Winnie. I wasn't interested in her before we got married, and I'm even less interested now. What's this really about?"

But he knew. It was about the marine. It had to be, right? It was about her looking for an out…an escape clause, a way to end things because she was probably still in love with the jerk who'd abandoned her at the altar, and still missed him.

"I...don't know. I...can't. I'm so—"

"Unhappy?" he said, cutting her off. "Yeah, I can see that. You were talking to Ellie."

"I needed someone to talk to and she's my friend."

"Sure," he said, understanding completely. And he didn't have any problem with her confiding in his sister, other than the one obvious point—it meant she wasn't confiding in him. Like they used to do. "Are you finished here for the day?" he asked.

She nodded. "Yeah, I'm tired. I think I need to go home and lie down."

"Okay, I'll see you back at the apartment later on. I'm going to drop by Joss's place for a while."

"Is everything all right?"

Grant nodded. "Fine."

He waited for her to lock up, escorted her to her car and then they headed in separate directions. He didn't kiss her, didn't touch her. He drove directly to his brother's and Joss answered the door quickly.

"Why do you look like you haven't slept for two days?" his brother asked as he crossed the threshold.

Grant rubbed the back of his neck. "Because I haven't."

"Beer?"

"Coffee," he replied. "Strong."

They headed to the kitchen and Joss quickly made coffee, told him the girls were having a sleepover at the ranch because they were having a horse-riding lesson with Mitch the next morning.

"They like hanging out with Tess," he said and shrugged. "It's the mothering thing, I guess. And Sissy's at that age where she needs female advice. Dad just doesn't cut it when it comes to talking about bras and monthly cycles and stuff."

Grant managed a grin. "Do you think you'll get married again?"

"I don't know. I know the girls would like me to. But I don't mix my love life with the parenting thing, you know. Too complicated. I don't want them getting attached to someone and then find myself screwing it up. Let's face it, Lara was a saint and I'm not sure I'll ever find someone who could put up with me like she did—and someone who'll also love the girls unconditionally."

"Oh, I don't know," Grant said and drank some coffee. "You're a lovable guy. And an understandable one."

Joss stilled and regarded him curiously. "What's going on?"

"I saw Billie-Jack yesterday."

His brother's eyes bulged as he swore. "You did what?"

"For about ten minutes," he replied and sucked in a long breath. "He's sick."

Joss pushed back on his heels, taking in the information. "Sick?"

"Dying, is my guess," Grant replied. "He didn't say that, but I suspect it's terminal."

The flash of angry shock in his brother's eyes faded. "How did this come about?"

"He called again, I picked up," he answered evenly. "I thought there was little point in avoiding it forever."

"What does he want? Money?"

"Amends," Grant replied, suddenly weary from thinking and talking about it. "Money would be easier."

Joss sighed. "Have you told anyone else?"

"No."

"Not even your wife?"

"Winnie and I don't talk much these days. We've perfected the art of not saying what's on our minds."

"I thought you said she wanted a divorce?"

He shrugged. "We're trying this new sixty-day arrangement, you know, to see if we can figure it out." Although since neither of them had signed the divorce papers yet, the plan was already busted.

"Sounds complicated," Joss said and smiled ruefully. "And you know what, marriage shouldn't be complicated. It should be the smartest thing you've ever done. You should be the best version of yourself with that person."

He finished his coffee, ignoring the ache settled behind his ribs that seemed to be a permanent fixture. "So, about Billie-Jack, I thought I'd start with you—are you interested in reconnecting?"

Joss didn't hide his skepticism. "You're, what, the envoy now?"

"Looks like it. It was probably a stupid move to meet him, but I was curious."

"Is your curiosity now satisfied?" Joss asked. "Because it doesn't seem like it is."

"I don't think so," he replied candidly. "I have a lot of questions I'd like answered. About why he started drinking so heavily after mom died. About why he'd beat up on you and Hank the most. And about the day of the accident, when he knew he was drunk but drove, anyway, with two of his kids in the vehicle. I want to know why he didn't pull Hank free of the wreck. And I want to know why he hasn't made any contact until now."

"You want a lot. If I remember correctly, didn't he send you a postcard about five years ago?"

"Yes," Grant replied. "Just postmarked from Arizona and his initials on it."

"He must have thought we cared where he was," Joss said. "Let's face it, we were all grateful to see the back of him."

Grant didn't respond. Because back then, at twelve years old, he *wasn't* happy to see his father go. He'd raced after him that day, begging him to stay, and then begging Billie-Jack to take him with him. No one knew that. Afterward, he'd been too ashamed to admit as much to his brothers.

"Does that mean you don't want to see him?" he asked.

"I don't think so," Joss replied. "I need to think about it."

"Are you pissed because I did?" he asked flatly.

"A little," his brother admitted honestly. "But I understand. Let me talk to Hank—since we're twins, he'll probably prefer to hear this from me."

Grant agreed. "Sure. I'll tell the others over the weekend."

"Don't forget the party on Sunday," Joss reminded him. "It's in your honor, remember?"

He remembered. But he wasn't looking forward to being center stage at a celebration for a marriage that was becoming more strained every day. He stayed at his brother's place for a while longer, heading back to Winnie's apartment around seven thirty. The kitchen light was on, but that was all, and he noticed she was lying on her side on the sofa, wearing a bathrobe, fast asleep. He spotted a plate and mug on the kitchen counter and a candy wrapper on the coffee table in front of the sofa. At least she'd eaten something and was resting.

He settled himself in the love seat opposite and saw her eyes spring open. "Hey, did I wake you?"

She pushed herself up onto one elbow. "No, I wasn't really sleeping, just dozing. Thank you for the flowers," she said as her mouth curved a little. "They're lovely. Unexpected, since flowers are generally not your style."

"I've given you flowers before."

"Once," she corrected. "When I was sixteen."

It was meaningless talk, the kind he knew was said to fill the silences between them. "I wanted to assure you that absolutely nothing happened with Krystal while I was in Duluth. I was there to work, and actually I hardly saw her."

"You don't need to—"

"Well, clearly I do," he said, cutting her off, "since you asked about her. I wouldn't do that to anyone," he added. "And I certainly wouldn't do that to you. Know that whatever happens between us, I would never dishonor you like that."

"I know. I overreacted. But I am committed to this marriage."

Grant dropped his gaze for a second. Because he couldn't—wouldn't—look in her eyes and see the lie in them. "I'm going to take a shower and make it an early night," he said and got to his feet.

Twenty minutes later he was showered, shaved, and he walked into Winnie's bedroom. She was in bed, sitting up against the pillows, wearing a long college T-shirt, her dark hair tumbling around her shoulders.

"I really am sorry about before," she said and pulled back the covers on his side, clearly inviting him into the bed. "About Krystal. My emotions have been seesawing all over the place lately."

Grant hovered in the doorway. He saw the gleam in her eye and wondered if she knew how sexy she looked with her tumbling hair and lips so naturally red she looked like she had already been kissed thoroughly. But he hadn't kissed her. He didn't dare. Because the way he was feeling, the way his heart was pounding, he knew he would betray and humiliate himself. He'd beg her to forget about the marine and think only of them...of *him*.

"Forget about it," he said and slipped into bed beside her, trying not to touch her.

But as he flicked off the bedside light, she curled up against him. It would have been easy to take up the invitation he knew she was offering...to roll her over and kiss her luscious mouth, to slide his tongue around her tightly budded nipples, to touch her intimately and hear her come apart at the gentle rhythm he knew she liked. Perhaps her acquiescence was a peace offering, an olive branch, a way of making amends for almost accusing him of doing whatever with another woman. The invisible wall he'd heard her talk about to his sister seemed higher than ever. She was going to try, obviously, despite their marriage feeling like something she had to endure.

Her hand slipped beneath the tank shirt he wore and rested in between his pecs, her fingers twirling through his chest hair. It was erotic and at the same time hypnotic, and his breathing quickly changed from rapid to restful.

"What time are you leaving in the morning?" she asked softly.

"Early. I said I'd be at the hos—" He stopped, holding on to the truth. "At the appointment at nine."

"What kind of appointment?"

He hesitated for a moment. "Just...work."

Grant had called Billie-Jack a couple of hours after their meeting at the café and said he would see him the following day at the hospital where he was receiving treatment. There were still things unsaid between them. And he wanted answers. He *needed* answers before he spoke to the rest of his siblings.

Lethargy climbed over his limbs and his mind wandered. Before his relationship with Winnie had gotten so complicated, he wouldn't have hesitated in confiding in her. They would have talked it through. She would have made him see the situation from all angles, not just his own. That's what pained him— that he didn't trust their *new* relationship enough to share what he was feeling.

And he wondered if he ever would.

Chapter Eleven

Grant left early the following morning and Winona heaved a sigh of relief the moment he walked out the door. He seemed so far away, so distant and cold. Not the man she was used to. But the man he'd become since Vegas.

And she was sadder than she had ever imagined she could be.

He'd rejected her in bed. Sure, he hadn't pushed her away, but there was a remoteness in his response to her touch, an indifference that hurt soul-deep. Is that what they'd become? She'd been kidding herself the weekend before, playing the role of wife and lover and setting herself up for the biggest fall of her life. It was simply sex. Physical release. It didn't mean closeness. Sure, it felt like it at the time, when the mind was hazy in the afterglow of pleasure and everything seemed right in the world. But reality quickly set in.

Sex was not love.

Love was not sex.

All she had to do was learn to compartmentalize her feelings. Accept what she had and learn to live with the crumbs of a friendship and a marriage based on obligation and loyalty. Because she would have that, she was sure. He would play the role of her husband because he was honorable to the core and a good person. Grant wouldn't cheat. He would be generous and faithful. He would also be a considerate and passionate lover. But there would be a huge divide. A permanent line in the sand with their roles clearly laid out. Wife and mother. Husband and father. And a busted friendship lying in ruins at their feet.

But still, she wanted to try. She wanted the chance to get him to open up. She longed to show him how much they could have if he met her halfway.

Winona headed downstairs to pack a few boxes into her car to take to the Maple Street house when she spotted Grant's car still parked beside hers. And Grant perched on the end of the hood. He still looked so tired and she suspected he had gotten as little sleep as she had.

"I thought you had a secret appointment in Rapid City?" she asked, verbalizing her curiosity for the first time. Of course she'd considered all kinds of possible scenarios, none of which made any sense. A wedding ring didn't give her carte blanche on his movements and he was entitled to his privacy.

"I do," he said, his pallor oddly ashen. "Would you like to come with me?"

He looked directly at her as he spoke and Winona saw raw vulnerability in his expression and it quickly sliced right through her. He wanted her with him. Needed her, by the look on his face. It was enough to make her nod. "Okay, sure."

He nodded and within minutes her car was locked, and they were on their way.

"Where are we going?" she asked.

He exhaled heavily. "To see my father."

Winona gasped. Of all the things she might have expected him to say, seeing Billie-Jack was not one of them. She was about to ask another question when he explained that his father was in the hospital receiving treatment.

"I saw him on Thursday when I got back to Rapid City," he said. "We talked for a while. I was planning on seeing him again yesterday."

"Until I had an emotional breakdown and made you come home, right?"

"You didn't make me do anything," he said quietly. "But I still have some questions for him."

"How did you feel seeing him after so long?"

He glanced at her. "Like I was in a movie of someone else's life. Weird, detached, but drawn into it at the same time. And about twelve years old all over again."

"Have you told your family?"

"Only Joss."

"That's why you went there last night? What did he say?"

"Not much," he replied.

Unsaid words hung in the air and she pushed a little more. "Grant? Please. You can talk to me."

He exhaled. "The thing is, I feel guilty for wanting to know why he left, because I know the rest of my family don't care. They've moved on, forgotten about him, I guess."

"Well, you're younger and perhaps not as jaded," she suggested. "I know what it did to you when he left."

Winona didn't ask him why he'd turned the car around and come back to get her. He had his reasons. Moral support, perhaps. And really, as his wife, it was her job to be that support when he needed it. They did the rest of the trip in uneasy silence and she was relieved when they finally arrived in Rapid City. The hospital was in the center of town and he found a parking space easily. He held her elbow as they walked into the ward and down a long corridor. She felt the tension emanating from him and grasped his elbow reassuringly.

Winona had seen a lot of pictures of Billie-Jack Culhane, but he'd certainly changed over the years. He greeted them politely and Grant quickly introduced her.

"This is my wife, Winona," he said, and the older man nodded.

"You're Red's granddaughter," Billie-Jack said, his eyes wrinkled in the corners. "My son told me you'd recently married, congratulations."

It was strange, making small talk with someone who she knew had wreaked absolute havoc on his family nearly two decades ago. Now, Billie-Jack looked small and old and without any kind of power. There was medication being transfused into his arm and a water jug on the side table. There were a couple of cards next to the jug and a small bouquet of flowers. Whatever had transpired in his life since he left Cedar River, he'd obviously maintained a connection with someone.

"The cards are from my girlfriend, Mindy," the old man explained. "She doesn't live here—she's in Arkansas. I told her I was coming back to try and see my kids and she understood. I'm sure she'd rather I was back there continuing treatment, but this hospital is a good one."

He kept talking and she noticed how tightly coiled Grant was beside her, like a wound-up top ready to spin. Finally, he spoke.

"Why did you do it? Why did you drive that day? And why the hell did you leave Hank in the truck?"

Billie-Jack's faded green eyes shadowed over. "The truth is, I can't remember much about it. I remember driving, I remember you and Hank being in the truck, I remember Jake being on his motorbike behind me, but I don't remember much about the accident. I know I was drinking that day," he admitted and looked at them both. "I drank every day. After your mom died, I lost part of myself. I couldn't handle the pain day to day. Couldn't handle anything."

"You didn't try," Grant said flatly.

He took a sip of water. "Look, I ain't makin' excuses. I was no good back then. I was a drunk. I was a bad husband, and after she died, I beat up on my kids." He made the acknowledgment without any expectation of forgiveness. "I was weak and a crap father. But that day, I just remember being out of the car and hearing yelling. Jake was there, racing around the truck as it was on fire, and I remember seeing you on the ground, sitting on the grass," he said and looked at Grant. "In my head I knew Hank was still in the truck, but I kinda blacked out, and couldn't think straight. The booze, I suppose."

He gazed out the window for a moment, the years seeming to weigh on him heavily for a moment. Then he turned back to them, shaking his head. "Anyway, like I said, it's no excuse. I should have given my own life to get him out of the there—or at least died tryin'," he admitted sadly. "But I wasn't a good man back then. And a violent drunk isn't the kind of person who should be raisin' kids."

"And that's why you left?" Grant said, his voice so tight she knew each word was hard for him. "Because it was best for everyone?"

"I had to," Billie-Jack said. "And I knew Mitch

would look after you, because he had your mom's strength. I was no good for you all. I used to take the strap to the twins and Jake would get in the middle of it, trying to get me riled into hitting him instead. And I did most times. Sometimes I hit you, too. Do you remember that?"

Grant nodded. "I remember."

"You wanted me to take you with me," Billie-Jack said dully. "I know that. I saw you runnin' after me that day. But where I was going was no place for a kid. You were better off with your brothers and sister." He sighed. "Look, I didn't come here expecting that forgiveness was going to be easy to get. I know I screwed up. You all have every reason to hate me and I'd understand. But I wanted to try," Billie-Jack said, his voice cracking. "I've got a whole bunch of regrets behind me, but for the last ten years I've managed to live a decent life. I met Mindy, got a job working at a timber mill and made peace with the guy upstairs. I've also come to realize that it's the things in life I haven't done that I regret the most. That's why I'm here."

Winona felt Grant's hand reach for hers, his fingers tight. "You want forgiveness? It's not only mine to give," he said, and she could feel the intense pain vibrating through him.

Billie-Jack nodded. "I know…but it's a start."

Winona wasn't sure what she expected Grant to say. He looked somewhere within the past, perhaps somewhere within himself. And she recognized the polarized expression on his face. She'd witnessed it before—the morning she'd told him she was pregnant. Shock. Disbelief. Lack of control. Things that undid him. And she knew, in that moment, that she needed to hold on tight, to lead him to where she believed he wanted to go.

"Grant," she whispered, leaning close to him, speaking so only he could hear. "Do what feels right for *you*."

He met her gaze, his glittering green eyes boring through her with burning intensity. And he nodded, clutching her fingers, taking all the strength he needed. He backed up, making his way to the door, and she followed in his wake. If he didn't want closure, she would understand and support his decision. But when they reached the door, he turned, half shielding her, his focus suddenly and completely on the old man in the hospital bed.

"Okay," he said quietly. "You want forgiveness. Here you go—I forgive you for falling apart after mom died. I forgive you for beating up on us when you were drunk. I forgive you for failing to protect my brother when the truck was on fire. I forgive you for walking away and leaving us. And I forgive you for not taking me with you."

Each word was like a rock hitting the ground with a resounding thud.

"And now," Grant said, "it's over. Good luck to you. We're done."

The adrenaline, mixed with a dose of relief that was coursing through his body, was palpable, and as they headed to his apartment in Rapid City, Grant was so exhausted he felt as though he'd scaled a mountain. It was Winnie's suggestion they go to his apartment for a while instead of driving directly to Cedar River and he quickly agreed. He wanted a shower and a change of clothes; he wanted to wash away the tarnish of the last hour that seemed to be clinging to his skin.

But he was glad she was with him. He wasn't sure what had motivated him to turn the car around and return to Cedar River. He only knew he needed her like he needed air in his lungs.

"It feels hollow in here," she said when they walked into the place. She'd been in his apartment countless times, and had never much liked the smooth chrome, black and glass decor.

"Well, it hasn't been lived in much lately."

She jerked her gaze to his. "I wasn't being critical," she explained. "Just, you know, being me… finding fault in everything."

Grant looked at her. "That cut deep, did it?"

She shrugged loosely. "I know I'm not perfect. And I didn't mean to say something so hurtful."

"I guess we all say hurtful things sometimes."

"Not you," she said and gave a humorless laugh. "You don't say anything."

Grant's chest tightened. "I've always thought actions speak louder than words," he said, suddenly so weary he could barely stand up. "I'm gonna take a shower and get changed. Make yourself at home."

He disappeared upstairs and wandered around the master bedroom for a while, opening drawers, looking at all the things he needed to pack to transition to the Maple Street house. Maybe he should simply leave the apartment as it was, so he had a place to crash that was close to work.

Or maybe I know my marriage isn't going to make it...

The notion banged around in his head like a chant. Because he knew, deep down, what that meant. Part-time fatherhood. Seeing his child on the weekends. Exactly what he wanted to avoid when he'd insisted that they stay married. Instead, Winnie had suggested they go ahead with the divorce, before then putting a time frame on their marriage to see if they could fumble through and make it work. They were a couple of weeks down and already he felt the strain and knew she did, too.

Because she's probably still in love with someone else...

And what was worse? Being together out of some old-fashioned sense of doing the right thing? Sleeping in the same bed, reaching for one another in the dark to feed a physical hunger, out of little more than duty and guilt? How long would it be before the cracks started to show? Wouldn't it be better to raise their child apart, with respect and friendship? It seemed like the healthier alternative.

Perhaps that's what they should have planned all along. His ideals about having some kind of happily-ever-after seemed like a foolish pipe dream. What did he have to compare it to? Seeing Billie-Jack had galvanized something inside him. That it was okay to fail at something. He'd felt guilty most of his life because he hadn't experienced the same loathing his siblings did for their father. Grant was the one who'd wanted to go with him. Another pipe dream, as it turned out, but one he could finally live with.

He stripped off and headed for the shower. The steaming water felt good, cathartic, as it beat down, and he rested a forearm against the tiles, exhaling heavily.

"Do you want some company?"

Her jerked around and saw Winnie standing outside the shower cubicle, completely naked.

"Ah—what?"

She slid open the door and the steam escaped. "I figured you might need me," she said as she stepped into the shower, the water hitting her shoulders and running down her breasts. "To wash your back, maybe?"

"Is that all?"

"Whatever you want," she replied, the provocation in her voice unmissable.

He wanted to believe her. He *ached* to believe her. But the thought of making love to her when she was thinking about someone else cut through him like a shiny blade. "Sex doesn't fix things, you know?" He said the words more to himself than to her.

"I know," she said, water now plastering her hair

to her head. "But for whatever reason, you asked me to come with you today to do something that was incredibly difficult. You needed me. And right now, I think you still need me."

He inhaled sharply. "That's the damnable thing about you and me, Winnie. We've been friends so long I think it's blurred what we need from each other."

She pressed a hand to his chest. "Like last night when we were in bed? You were thinking about today, about Billie-Jack, about your family."

"I was thinking about a lot of things last night."

"You didn't want to make love to me," she said hollowly.

I did, so much... But he didn't say it. Instead, he looked at her, his body quickly responding to her skin, her hair, her hard nipples. He couldn't deny it, couldn't halt the primal reaction she evoked in him. Grant groaned and reached for her instinctively, wrapping his arms around her and finding her hot, wet mouth, which was so clearly eager for his kiss that his knees almost buckled. They kissed deeply, tongues and teeth clashing, like they were starved of one another. And her hands were everywhere—over his back, his thighs, his chest—her fingers hot and seeking. He wasn't sure how, but he lifted her up to his hips, one arm bracing them against the tiles, the other anchored around her waist, and slowly entered her. She clung to him, kissing his mouth, his neck, any place she could find as they settled into a fierce rhythm that quickly had them both free-falling into an abyss of pleasure so intense Grant wasn't sure his legs would hold out.

When it was over, he supported himself against the wall and gently set her back down, their labored breath mingled and testament to the passion they had just shared. So much for his earlier thoughts about respect and friendship. He was kidding himself. His libido had suddenly begun to rule him—one touch, one smile, and he couldn't control himself.

He wanted to resent her so much in that moment he could taste it. But instead, he turned the resentment into self-disgust at his own stupid male weakness.

"I'm not sure I can walk after that," he breathed into her hair, drifting down to nuzzle the tender spot at the base of her throat.

Her arms were still around his waist. "I wish we could stay like this forever," she said against his chest.

"We'd get all pruned after a while," he said, running his hands down her hips, loving the feel of the water cascading over her skin. "Thank you for coming with me today."

She smiled. "I'd do anything for you."

Except think of me as the man you really love...

He had no idea where that thought came from and it had nowhere to go but remain banging around in his head. He switched off the faucets and then they were quickly out of the shower. They dried off and got back in their clothes soon after.

"What do you plan on telling your brothers and sister about Billie-Jack?" she asked as they dressed.

"The truth," he replied. "And they can make whatever decision they choose."

"Did you mean what you said? About being done with him?"

Grant's hands stilled on his belt buckle. "I think so. I needed to hear it from him, you know, the admission that he screwed up. Hearing him say it switched off something inside—something I've been hanging on to for years."

"What's that?"

"Fear," he admitted. "Of screwing up. Of checking out when things get difficult. Of making the easy choice instead of the hard one."

"That doesn't sound like you."

"Doesn't it?" he shot back and slipped on his shoes. "I was the one who insisted we stay married because of the baby. If I remember correctly, you believed we could successfully co-parent our child without the wedding ring."

"I know, but I—"

"What if you were right?" he asked, tired of the pretense, tired of her *trying* so hard. "And maybe I said we should stay married because it was the easy option and it would mean we weren't as screwed up as our parents."

"We'll never know, I guess."

"I'd rather not leave it to chance," he said quietly.

"I don't want to make the wrong the decision now, and risk hurting my kid down the track."

Grant sighed, seeing her building distress and knowing he could do nothing for her. He wanted to hold her and protect her from the world and everyone in it. He wanted to be the kind of husband and father he witnessed his brothers Mitch, Jake and Joss being. But he couldn't because of one indisputable fact—Winnie was still in love with someone else. She might make love with him as though they were the only two people in the world, but beneath that facade was the truth he knew she couldn't fake—her heart was broken and there was no room in it for anything other than sex, obligation and duty.

"I think it's time we both accepted the truth. This marriage is never going to work."

Winona stared at him, fighting the heat suddenly burning behind her eyes. They'd just shared the most intense and erotic lovemaking of her life and now he was saying they were done?

"I don't understand," she said rawly. "I thought you wanted us to—"

"At this point I don't think it matters what I want," he said, cutting her off. "Let's face it, Winnie, this situation isn't one either of us ever imagined we'd be in."

I did, she cried to herself. *I dreamed it. I longed for it.*

"But we just…" Her words trailed off as she gestured toward the bathroom. "You know."

"Didn't we establish that sex doesn't fix things?"

Pain seared through her. "I guess I imagined it would be enough."

"For how long? Six months? A year or two? Until the novelty wears off and we realize that's *all* we've become—two people who are great in bed together. Do you really think that's enough? And when it's not, do you think that's fair on our child, Winnie?"

Nothing was fair. Particularly not the cold, uncompromising way he was looking at her. Half an hour ago they were in the middle of something so intimate, so erotic, it defied belief. Now he regarded her as though they were nothing to each other.

"I'm not sure I know anything anymore."

He sighed with a kind of heavy resignation. "I'm tired of pretending we can make this work. Whatever you think we have here…it's not enough. I want… more."

He strode to the dressing table, pulled open the drawer and extracted a large envelope. He pulled out the contents, grabbed a pen from the bedside table and quickly scribbled his name on the appropriate page.

"There," he said and dropped the pages onto the bed. "Our divorce papers. All you have to do is sign and it can be finalized. I know it's what you want, Winnie."

He left the room and, once he was out of sight, Winona dropped onto the bed and picked up the papers with a shaking hand. And then, in the quiet of the room, sadness overtook her. She felt about fifteen all over again. Like the girl who'd pined over him for years, dreaming about having his love but never quite believing she would ever get it.

Confusion settled in her chest and she splayed a hand across her belly. Maybe in time the hurt would lessen. Perhaps she'd find someone else to love, who would love her. But it didn't seem likely. He said he wanted more—but what did that mean? Had he come to realize that he wanted a relationship...or even love? Did he believe he'd be *settling* if they gave their marriage a chance?

Her sense of rejection was consuming and soul-crushing, but the tears she wanted to shed wouldn't come. Her throat ached, her fingers were numb, and she could barely catch her breath...but she *wouldn't* fall apart. Not here, in the cold bedroom of his soulless apartment.

She tucked the papers into her tote and headed downstairs, spotting him by the front door.

"We should get going," she said quietly, too hurt to say much else.

He nodded and, once the apartment was locked up, they headed back to Cedar River. The silence between them was thick, tense and worse than she could have imagined. When they arrived outside the bakery he moved to get out of the car, but she put up a hand.

"No, don't," she said dismissively. "You should

stay somewhere else tonight. Maybe Joss's. Or the hotel. Just not here."

"Of course," he said, his fingers tight on the steering wheel. "We have that thing at the ranch tomorrow, remember?"

Oh, God, the party. Winona had forgotten all about it. She remembered the two missed calls she had on her cell from Ellie and guilt immediately pressed down on her shoulders. "We need to cancel. I can't possibly go."

"It's a little late to cancel, don't you think? Look, I don't want to be a part of it any more than you do, but Ellie and Tess have gone to a lot of trouble, so we should probably fake it a little longer and try to make out like everything is okay. We can wait a week or so to tell everyone anything different."

"Lie, you mean?"

He glanced at her, his green eyes icy cold. "All right, I'll call Tess and tell her we're—"

"No," she said quickly, cutting him off. "You're right. We'll get through tomorrow like it's business as usual. I do think we should talk about the house, though, since we've just signed a lease."

"The house is yours to live in, Winnie. Once the baby is born, I'll drive down as often as I can and bunk at the ranch or stay with one of the twins."

He had it all figured out—clearly.

"Great, I'll see you at the ranch at three o'clock tomorrow."

"I'll pick you up," he said quietly.

"I'll drive myself," Winona insisted as she opened the door.

His hand touched her arm, gently holding her. "Winnie, I don't want us to hurt each other."

She stilled, shrugging off his touch. "Too late."

Then she headed up to her apartment, dropped onto the sofa and cried until she was all out of tears.

Chapter Twelve

"You're what?"

Grant glanced at his brother. "Getting a divorce."

He was sitting on the couch in Joss's living room later that night, after calling each of his siblings to explain about Billie-Jack. Considering everything that had happened, they all took the news reasonably well. Grant didn't offer any suggestions, or try to negotiate a meeting with their father; he simply relayed the facts. He didn't expect any of them to see the old man, and frankly, he didn't much care. He couldn't control how they dealt with it and it wasn't his job to make amends on Billie-Jack's behalf. That settled, now he was sipping a beer he didn't really want, watching a baseball game he had little interest in. And he really didn't want to get into the details of his failed marriage. But since over the last hour they'd exhausted the topic of Billie-Jack, Grant knew his brother would want to have a discussion about Winnie.

"Ah, didn't we have the marriage-shouldn't-be-complicated talk yesterday?"

"Yeah. Things change."

"This is kind of a record speed," Joss said, brows up. "What happened?"

"Good sense prevailed," he said and stared at the television. When his brother didn't respond, he looked up. "Six weeks ago, she was going to marry someone else."

"And?"

"And we got drunk, got married and got laid. It's not supposed to happen like that."

"Oh, there's a set plan for marriage, is there?" Joss inquired, clearly amused.

"There should be."

Joss chuckled. "Like me getting my high school girlfriend pregnant at eighteen and then getting married as a teenager, and then being a widower at twenty-three?"

"You loved Lara."

"I did," Joss agreed. "I still do. That doesn't mean we didn't make mistakes along the way. So, this idea about what relationships should be—enlighten me."

Grant scowled. "I don't know…just not like this."

Joss's brows shot up. "Maybe like Mitch and

Tess—get married, have a series of tragic miscarriages, get divorced, hook up randomly a few years later, get pregnant and get married again?" Joss offered, grinning a little. "Or Jake and Abby—date in high school, he joins the military while she marries his best friend, best friend dies, he comes back to town, knocks her up and finds out he has a son six years later? Yeah," Joss said and grinned. "I see what you mean—your situation is way more convoluted. Do you love her?"

"That's a stupid question," he said and scowled some more. "It's Winnie, of course I love her."

His brother tutted. "I mean, are you *in love* with her?"

Grant averted his gaze from the television and looked at Joss. "There's a difference?"

"Of course there's a freakin' difference. I love her, too," he said impatiently. "We all love her. But *you're* the one who married her and got her pregnant."

Grant ignored the twitch in his gut and the bluntness of his brother's words. He knew exactly what he had done. "She still loves the marine."

"You know that for sure?"

"Yes," he replied dully.

"You didn't answer the question," Joss said quietly. "About being in love with her."

Grant's temple throbbed. He didn't want to answer the question. He didn't want to think about Winnie and the desolate look on her face as she raced from his car. He wasn't sure he'd ever get that look out of his mind.

"I'm not sure I know what that even means."

Joss shook his head. "Man, you really are screwed up, aren't you?"

"Just because I'm not falling in and out of love on a regular basis, it doesn't make me a screwup. I care about Winnie," he said and got to his feet, striding back and forth. "So yeah, I love her, okay. Of course I do. She's my best friend."

"That's all?" Joss asked.

He stilled. "That's everything."

And then, suddenly, as he said the words, it all made sense. His rage, his resentment, his never thinking any man was good enough for her; the bone-aching jealousy he experienced every time he thought about the man she'd almost married. And the other things—the pleasure of her touch, her kiss, the way making love to her transcended all rational thought. The way he couldn't talk to anyone the way he could talk to her. Not even his brothers, even though he'd never admit it to them.

"I feel like I have this great weight pressing in my chest," he admitted, running a hand through his hair. "Almost like it's twisting inside my rib cage. Is that…" His voice trailed off and he shrugged. "Is that it?"

Joss grinned. "You mean being in love? You feel like crap, you can't eat, you can't sleep. Yeah, that would be it."

Grant's shoulders dropped. He'd loved Winnie since they were kids…and somehow, in the last few tumultuous weeks, something incredible had happened—he'd fallen in love with his best friend. It was like a light had been switched on inside him. He also remembered what he'd done just a few hours earlier. He'd said they shouldn't hurt one another, and she replied that it was too late. Was she hurting like he was?

"I signed the divorce papers today," he said.

"Nothing that can't be undone," Joss remarked.

"Maybe…but…the marine…"

"Is she still in contact with him?" Joss asked, all big-brotherly.

Grant shook his head, feeling about twelve years old. "I don't think so. Except in here," he added and tapped his chest.

Joss stood and slapped him affectionately on the shoulder. "Get some sleep. And tomorrow, do yourself a favor and go and talk to your wife."

Sleep would have been great. He couldn't quite remember the last time he'd slept through the night. Was it really only a week ago? When he'd had her arms wrapped around him.

Grant tossed and turned most of the night and woke up early. He went for a run, ate breakfast with his brother and nieces and tried to act normal around his family. But what he really wanted to do was tap on Winnie's door at 8:00 a.m. and beg for her to give them another chance—even though he was the one who'd signed the divorce papers.

He waited until ten and drove to her apartment. However, she wasn't there. He asked at the bakery and Regina informed him she hadn't seen Winnie that morning. He tried her cell and it went to messages. He sent a text and didn't get a return message. He held out for about twenty minutes, pacing the street outside the bakery. Still nothing. He took a chance and drove to the house on Maple Street, but there was no sign she'd been there that morning.

Grant lingered outside for a few minutes, thinking how warm and welcoming the place looked. In a flash of a few seconds, he saw his life so clearly—his car parked in the driveway, Winnie greeting him on the porch with a gentle smile, a couple of kids racing around the yard, a shaggy dog playing chase with a stick. It seemed so real it rendered him breathless. If he inhaled he'd pick up the scent of her perfume mixed with the aroma of the cookies she loved to bake. He could almost hear their kids laughing, calling him Daddy, clearly delighted he was home. And Winnie—her beautiful eyes meeting his with the promise of what was to come when they were finally alone after dinnertime was done and their children were asleep. The image polarized him; the memory of things that hadn't even happened yet struck him with such force he could barely breathe.

He pushed some life into his legs, got back into his car and drove to the ranch.

And the first thing he saw when he arrived was her orange VW parked outside her grandfather's cottage. He pulled up in front of the main house and walked up the path between the dwellings. She was on the small porch, hands on hips, wearing jeans and a bright pink T-shirt, her beautiful hair hanging around her shoulders, before he made it to the bottom step.

"The party isn't until three," she said, her cheeks flushed with color.

"I know," he replied and kicked absently at a rock on the ground. "I thought we should talk."

"I haven't signed the divorce papers yet," she hissed. "If that's what you're wondering. But I will. The quicker we finish this, the better."

He could see the hurt in her expression. "Is that what you really want?"

"It's what *you* want," she reminded him. "You were the one who tossed them in my face right after we made love, remember? Nice going, by the way, very considerate."

Guilt, and a good dose of shame, pushed down squarely on his shoulders. "I'm sorry... I wasn't thinking straight. I was—"

"And why did you do this?" she asked brittlely, cutting him off as she shook her left hand. "Why did you insist we buy new wedding rings if this was the plan all along?"

"It wasn't the plan," he replied. "But you—"

"Why did you say we should get a house? Make

me believe we were going to, I don't know, *try*? Why did you kiss me? Touch me? Make love to me?" She fired out the questions so fast he didn't have a chance to reply. "Why did you pretend that you wanted me?"

Grant rocked back on his heels. "I wasn't pretending."

"No," she said with a tight, disbelieving laugh. "Then what changed? Last weekend everything seemed so right…like we were happy. And then yesterday, you asked me to go with you to see your father and I thought that meant something."

"It did," he assured her. "I needed you."

"You needed me?" she echoed, her eyes glittering. "For what? One last hookup? I know I was the one who initiated our little shower scene, but you didn't exactly take a lot of convincing. Any *body* would have done, I guess."

"Don't say that," he said, hating the way she made it sound so casual. "It's just that I was… I don't know…pissed, okay. I was mad at you for what you said the other day."

"What I said?" she repeated. "I don't understand."

"That you missed *him*," he said, each word clawed from his throat. "The marine. I heard you when you were talking to my sister. You said you missed him, and you were heartbroken."

She shook her head, searing him with an incredulous expression. "That's what you heard? That's *all* you heard?"

"I heard enough."

She laughed humorlessly. "I wasn't talking about Dwight," she said, the sound of the other man's name making him twitch. "I was talking about *us*. I was talking about you!"

"Me?" he echoed in disbelief.

"Are you that wrapped up in yourself that you can't figure it out?" she demanded, tears falling from her eyes. "You really are unbelievable, Grant. Do me a favor and go straight to hell," she said before she walked back inside and slammed the door.

He stayed where he was for a few minutes, feeling like a heel, a fool and a coward.

"Give her some time to calm down, son."

Grant saw Red to his left and realized the older man had heard most, if not all, of the entire exchange. He took a long breath. "I am in love with her, you know. For real."

Red nodded. "I know. Just let her cool down for a while—you know she's got a quick temper."

He knew that. He did, too. But he was better at keeping it under wraps. Grant managed a tight smile and walked back to the main house. Tess was there, and Ellie, and they were busy in the kitchen with Mrs. B, making preparations for the small gathering they were having that afternoon. Only family and a couple of close friends, thank goodness, because Grant wasn't sure he could stand anything more. But there were gifts and a cake set up on a long sideboard in the main dining room. Mitch tried to talk to him in the hallway about something and he brushed off his brother's conversation because his head, heart and insides hurt so much he couldn't concentrate on anything other than the thought of being miserable because Winnie had told him to take a hike.

He looked out of the window, noticing things about the ranch he hadn't spared much time to look at over the years. Like the flower beds. And the garden ornaments he figured his brother had bought for Tess because he knew she liked that kind of thing. He'd never been one to envy others, but in that moment, he did. He envied how easy Mitch and Tess made it look. He envied that Joss could still talk about Lara, even though he obviously missed her, and that Jake was so open about how much his wife and son meant to him. He envied emotional honesty because he'd always been too afraid to allow himself to feel it.

"I said I was heartbroken because I've lost the most important thing in my life."

Grant turned on his heel and saw Winnie standing in the doorway, clutching a small, faded and well-worn purple book. She was breathing hard, like every word caused her pain.

"Winnie, I—"

"Our friendship," she explained quietly. "Which has always meant more to me than anything else. But since Vegas, we've lost that, and I feel that loss so deeply I almost can't bear thinking about it. That's what's killing me, knowing we've lost what we had."

He swallowed the emotion burning in his throat. "It's not lost. I'm right here."

"No, you're not," she refuted. "Oh, you've been trying at times, like I have, but nothing is the same as it used to be. And the thing is, a part of me is glad. Because I'm really happy about the baby and I can't wait to be a mom—but I know it's come at a huge price."

"What price?"

"You and me. Our incredible friendship," she replied. "Which I've always treasured. Because I've always treasured you."

The way she said the words made him draw in a sharp breath. He wanted to believe her...so much. "But the marine...six weeks ago he was the love of your life."

"I never said that," she replied softly.

"Then why were you going to marry him?"

Her eyes glistened. "Because you never asked me."

Stunned, he stood still, unable to move if he tried.

"This is my diary," she said, her voice so raw it cracked. "I started writing in it when I was thirteen. I stopped writing in it when I finished high school. In this book I poured all of my heart, my thoughts and deepest feelings. Read it," she instructed. "And you'll see how there's only one man that I've ever loved."

She dropped the book on the sofa and left the room.

Grant wasn't sure how long he stood there for—minutes. Long enough for him to see Winnie's VW career down the driveway in a cloud of dust and grit through the window. He looked at the book, almost too afraid to pick it up. But he did. He held it in shaking hands, sat down and started reading.

Dear Diary,
I can't stop thinking about him. I know I'm dreaming. I know Grant will never look at me as anything more than a friend. But I love him so much. I want to marry him one day.

His heart raced. But he kept reading. Kept absorbing every word.

Dear Diary,
Grant came back from college this weekend and bought me flowers for my birthday. I'm going to press the roses into a book and carry them in my wedding bouquet when we get married.

All this time. Emotion lodged firmly in his throat and he flicked the page, and then another. The pain, the angst, the tortured teenage yearning of a girl clearly in love—it tugged at him so profoundly he blinked back the burning in his eyes.

Dear Diary,
Grant brought a girl to the ranch today. She was pretty and smiled a lot and I think he likes her. I wanted to die. I wish I had the courage to tell him to wait for me to grow up. Diary, I love

him so much. I'll always love him. I just hope that one day he realizes that he loves me, too.

Grant felt the wetness on his cheeks well before he realized he was crying. Damn. He wiped at his face as he read some more, the ache in his chest so intense he could barely draw a breath.

Dear Diary

Callum kissed me today. But he's not who I wanted to kiss. I was thinking about Grant the whole time. I don't think I'll ever love anyone else the way I love him. I dream about him all the time. I dream about getting married and having babies with him one day. I want three kids, two boys and a girl. I know I have to forget my silly dreams, because he's never going to think about me that way, but I honestly don't know if I can.

He closed the book and sucked in a long breath. All this time. Years. She'd loved him. *Him.* And he'd been too foolish to see it. Too blinded by old fears of abandonment that he'd tried to deep-freeze his feelings. Grant got to his feet, pushed back his shoulders and exhaled.

"Is everything all right?"

He looked around and saw Ellie and Mitch in the door. "Everything's going to be fine."

Neither sibling looked convinced. "Isn't that Win's old diary?" Ellie asked curiously.

Grant nodded and tucked the book under his arm. "Yeah."

"She let you read it?" his sister asked, eyes bulging.

It was obvious Ellie knew exactly what was written in the tattered notebook. "You knew?"

"Of course I knew. Everybody knew...and knows. Except you, I'm guessing," she added. "Where *is* Win?"

"I'm not sure. But wherever she is, she's mad as hell at me." He pulled his car keys from his pocket. "I'll be back. Don't start the party without us."

"Where are you going?" Ellie asked as he strode out of the room.

"To go find my wife and beg her to forgive me for being an idiot," Grant said as he passed them.

Winona wasn't sure why she fled to the Maple Street house. She should have gone home to her apartment. But the big house drew her, and she wanted to see it one last time. Because she absolutely would not be living in the place without her husband. She'd stay at her apartment. Or go and live with her grandfather. Or find somewhere else where every room wouldn't be sure to remind her of her broken dreams. Because the big house with the chokecherry tree in the yard and perfect window seat in the living room was not going to be where she spent her days and nights pining after a man who was obviously determined to divorce her and raise their child separately.

Well, if that's what he wanted, that's what he'd get.

Because she could do it. She felt strong and resilient and empowered by the truth of her own words. Admitting her feelings to Grant had switched on something inside her—resolve. And the determination to raise her child as a single mom. She didn't have to screw it up like her own mother had. She had a job and a support network of family and friends. She wasn't her mother. She didn't need to be married. And she knew Grant would be a good father to their child. He just sucked at being a husband.

Winona walked around the house for over half an hour, going from room to room, memorizing the wallpaper and the architraves, the intricately detailed ceiling that rose in the main stairwell and the ornate fireplace in the living room. She lingered in the kitchen, and then again upstairs, forging images in her mind of a nursery she knew she wouldn't have, but it still gave her comfort to dream a little. Finally, when her emotions were spent and she'd had enough wallowing in what-ifs, she headed back downstairs to collect her tote.

And saw Grant standing by the window seat in the empty room.

He met her startled gaze and she noticed her diary in his hand. "I worked out why I can't sleep these days."

Winona held her breath, her heart thundering. "Why?"

"Because talking to you at night, right before I go to bed, has always been like a kind of tonic. The kind that makes me forget any troubles, any stresses. I miss hearing you say that you love me," he said raggedly, swallowing hard. "Turns out, I need that because it's the only thing that soothes my soul."

"Is it really?" she dared ask, shocked by his admission. It was the closest he'd ever come to truly admitting anything.

He nodded. "And I worked out why I hate the marine, and that jerk from high school, and any other guy you've dated."

"You have?"

"Because I was crazy jealous," he admitted. "I didn't know what it was at the time. That's because I'm afraid of real intimacy, which I'm sure you know."

"That's quite a confession," she said softly, her emotions banging all over the place.

His mouth pressed into a tight line. "Do you want more?"

"I want it all," she replied.

He nodded fractionally, then let out a long and weary breath. "I love you, Winnie."

She gasped and then steeled herself. "I know you do. But—"

"And not that thoughtless *ditto* thing I've been saying to you for years," he said and dropped the diary on the window seat. "I know now that my actions, my responses, were never enough. Never what you deserved. Because despite my stupid behavior, despite acting as foolish as I have for so long, I promise you that with all my heart I'm absolutely and completely in love with you."

And then, without warning, he dropped to one knee and looked up at her.

"Grant, I—"

"This is how I should have done it," he said rawly. "Long before now. Winnie, will you marry me?"

Stunned, she stared at him for a moment, and then stated the obvious, her heart beating an erratic tattoo. "We're already married."

"I mean, marry me again, at the ranch, or in the chapel in town, or even at the courthouse if you like," he said quickly, urgently, like he couldn't get the words out fast enough. "I just know I want to do it again, with our family and friends around. A real wedding and a honeymoon and all the beauty and joy that you deserve."

Winona's heart was racing so hard she was sure he could hear it. He looked so raw, so vulnerable, and she quickly melted. She walked across the room and stood in front of him and he wrapped his arms around her, burying his face into her belly. Winona touched his head, threading fingers through his hair, feeling him tremble against her.

"Yes, I'll marry you," she whispered. "Again."

He kissed her stomach over and over, splaying his hands across her belly. "Thank you. God, I love that we've made a baby together."

He couldn't have said a more beautiful thing if he tried. Winona tugged on his shoulder and urged him to his feet. "That was kind of romantic, you know," she said and pressed against him. "On one knee and everything."

"I can be romantic," he assured her. "I promise to try harder."

"You don't have to," she replied and led him to the window seat. "Just be yourself."

"You mean, overcautious, commitment phobic and borderline predictable."

"Yes," she said and smiled, happiness tightening her chest. "I love all those things about you."

He glanced at the diary between them and grasped her chin. "Yeah, I kind of figured that."

"Silly schoolgirl dreams," she whispered.

"It was very sweet," he assured her again, holding her gently. "Made me cry actually."

Winona's throat burned and her brows shot up. She knew what that admission would have cost him. "Really? You never cry."

"I know," he admitted. "But I've decided I'm not going to be one of those fathers who tells his sons to stop blubbering and man-up."

"Like your father did?"

He nodded. "Yeah. I think that's part of the reason I hold back from admitting how I feel about things. Well, the way I *used* to hold back. From now on, I promise I will always be honest about what I'm feeling."

"Grant," Winona said, reaching up to hold his face in her hands. "I know that about you. You're my best friend...and best friends know that stuff."

"So, I have no secrets?" he teased.

She shook her head. "None, I'm afraid. I know that you say *Gladiator* is your favorite movie, but it's actually *The Blues Brothers*. I know you became a vegetarian after one Thanksgiving when you saw my grandfather prepare the turkey from scratch," she said with a grimace. "I know that you have a quick temper but you're such a control freak you always manage to keep it under wraps."

"Except when I think about you almost marrying that marine," he admitted.

Then he kissed her—a loving and tender kiss that literally made her insides sing. Winona kissed him back with every ounce of love she had been holding in her heart.

"Grant," she said in between kisses, "about Dwight..."

"I'd rather not talk about him, you know."

"Just for a moment, and then we'll forget all about

it, I promise. I suspect you're curious about why I accepted his proposal?"

"You told me," he replied, "because I didn't ask you."

She smiled, loving him so much she had trouble drawing in a breath. "It wasn't only that. I think I just wanted to belong, you know, to something or someone. And the long-distance relationship thing suited me, because I could be a part of something but still hang on to what I really wanted. Which was you, of course."

"I'm an idiot," he muttered.

She smiled. "And anyway, I guess it's a good thing in the end that he did leave me at the altar," she said and laughed softly. "Or otherwise we wouldn't be here right now."

He grasped her chin again, holding her steady, his touch gentle and loving. "Do you really think I would have stood by and let that happen?"

Winona's eyes widened. "What would you have done?"

"I don't know," he replied, kissing her cheek, her neck, the tender spot below her ear. All the places she loved to be kissed. "But I'd have figured something out. Because when I think about it, I realize that even then, I always knew he wasn't the guy for you."

"You did?"

"Sure," he said, still kissing her neck. "The thought

of losing you made me realize how much I needed you. Because I love you," he said, now against her lips. "So much."

"Ditto," she breathed and then smiled.

He pulled back a little, meeting her gaze. "Yeah… I'm not going to be saying that anymore, okay?"

Winona grinned. "Just every now and then," she teased. "And for the record, when we were in Vegas at the chapel, I was secretly hoping you wouldn't let me go ahead and marry him."

His gaze softened. "Why didn't you ever say anything?"

"Say what? And when—some opening in between your casual dating life?"

"Ouch," he said and smiled. "I am that predictable?"

"A little," she said. "But I understood. I know you didn't want to get too close to anyone. I know losing your mom, and then Billie-Jack leaving, closed off something inside. I guess I knew that because I understood loss—I understood what it meant to be left. So most of the time I tried not to think about what I really wanted because I didn't want to lose what we had. It's a lot, really. There were times when I thought it was enough."

"You know, even though we have all this…you'll always be the dearest friend I've ever had."

Happiness radiated through her. "I love you, Grant. So before, when you admitted you were a big crybaby," she teased again, "you said *sons*… Are you planning on more than our little peanut here?" she asked, touching her stomach.

Grant's large hand covered hers. "Well, I have read your diary, and I know all *your* secrets."

She sighed happily. "I'm so looking forward to being a mom. To having a family. To sharing that with my grandfather and your brothers and sister... and with you," she added.

"Me, too," he said, kissing her again. "And about this house...you really like it, don't you?"

She nodded. "So much. How did you know I'd be here?"

He shrugged. "I just knew. I drove by this morning looking for you, and realized you were right— this is the perfect place to raise our family."

"Do you think we could—"

"Absolutely," he said, gently cutting her off. "We'll talk to the Realtor and see if the owner is interested in selling sooner rather than later. We'll make an offer and go from there. I'll put my apartment on the market, and I also have a lot of money saved," he said, looking faintly embarrassed. "Enough for a generous deposit and some renovations and anything else you want. Like, we should probably buy a big SUV for all the kids."

"That would be sensible thing to do. We can put my VW in storage as a graduation gift for our first-born," she said and grinned. "And there is something else I've been thinking about."

"What's that?" he asked.

"The bakery," she replied. "I know Regina would love me to take up her partnership offer, and I thought that with the baby coming that I wouldn't be able to fit something else in, you know. But I think I can," she said, feeling strength seep through her bones. "I think I'm ready to live my real life. To stop being afraid of failure and do what I know will make me happy."

His arms tightened around her. "Of course you are. I'm so proud of you."

"I'm proud of *us*," she said and swooned a little.

He kissed her again, sighing against her mouth. "I can't believe I've missed out on kissing you and making love to you for all these years. I have a lot of time to make up."

She chuckled. "Yes, you do, Culhane."

"Ah, one thing," he said, pulling back a little. "Those…ah…papers I gave you yesterday. Do you have them?"

She nodded and grabbed her tote, extracting the documents with shaking hands. "I didn't sign them."

His jaw tightened. "I'm ashamed that I did," he said and gently took them from her. "I can't even begin to think how much that must have hurt you, and I'm sorry. Hurting you is the last thing I ever want to do. I have no excuse other than I was stupidly jealous and didn't think you wanted or loved…me."

"I've loved you since that first day I arrived at the ranch and you talked me down from the hayloft when we were kids," she admitted. "I've loved only you for most of my life."

He visibly shuddered. "I promise you, Winnie, with all my heart, that I will love you and cherish you for the rest of my life. I will always honor you and be faithful to you," he said and quietly tore up the paper in his hands and tossed it in the fireplace. "I'll be the kind of husband you deserve and a much better father than my own."

Winona looked at her husband—strong-willed, proud, stubborn, sometimes infuriating—and saw only the tender love in his expression. For her. For them. For their future. And she believed him to the depths of her heart.

"Grant, have you reconciled your feelings for Billie-Jack?" she asked gently.

"I'm not sure," he replied. "Some, probably not all. That will take time, I guess."

"I'll support whatever decision you make. I mean, if you do want to see him again, I'll go with you, be there and help you through it."

"I know. It was weird telling everyone about him—but also kind of like lancing this painful wound, almost cathartic. They can make their own minds up about what they want to do. It's not my job or place to tell anyone how to feel about things. When he first contacted me, I thought I was protecting them by keeping quiet. Turns out, I was only protecting myself because I felt guilty that I didn't quite hate him as much as everyone else."

Winona knew how much that statement cost him. Knew how achingly vulnerable the words made him feel. "You're allowed to love your father—even if it hurts."

He swallowed hard. "I know. But honestly, I'm tired of looking back. I only want to look forward from now on—and to our life together. We should get going," he suggested and held out his hand.

Winona touched his fingertips and was gently pulled into his embrace. "Where to?"

"The ranch," he replied. "We have a party to get to."

She smiled. In the midst of all she was feeling, Winona had forgotten about the get-together at the ranch. "They must all think I'm a lunatic racing off like that."

He chuckled. "You needed to give me a chance to come to my senses."

She didn't disagree. And she loved that he'd risked his heart and pride to come after her. "What shall we tell everyone?"

"The truth," he said and kissed her. "That we love each other very much. That we'll be together until we're old and gray. That we're gonna have a bunch of babies and live happily-ever-after."

She smiled. "I like the sound of that."

"Me, too," Grant said as he kissed her.

Winona kissed him back, knowing she had his love and commitment, knowing she had all she'd ever longed for.

And so much more.

Epilogue

A year later...

"You know, you can put her in her crib."

Grant cradled his daughter, Rorie, in the crook of his arm. "I know."

Winnie's beaming smile made his belly leap. "We'll never get everything done tonight."

"Sure we will," he assured her. "I've mastered the art of decorating those little cupcake things with one hand."

"Sweetie," she said and laughed, "our three-month-old daughter is better at cake decorating than you are."

He placed his free hand to his chest and touched the spot above his heart. "That's harsh."

"But true," she replied. "Anyhow, you have other talents."

Grant caught the gleam in her eyes and grinned. "Is that right?"

"Yes," she said and moved toward him, gently easing their sleeping child from his arm. "I need that shelf put up by the water cooler."

"Boss lady," he said and watched her for a moment as she placed Rorie in her crib. Grant never got tired of watching them, of seeing the love in Winnie's eyes for the baby who'd brought them together in a way he'd never imagined possible.

There were other things, too, that had made their relationship stronger over the past year. Like having a proper wedding surrounded by their family and friends. Like buying the house on Maple Street and making it their own, and Grant pulling back from traveling on business too much so he could spend more time with his family. And the bakery—which had been known as the Muffin Box for years and was now rebranded simply as Winnie's. As it turned out, Regina was happier to sell the place rather than take on a business partner, since she wanted to go on the road with her drummer boyfriend. And a couple of months earlier, after much consultation with an accountant, a lawyer and the bank, Winnie had made the decision to purchase the place for a fair price. After a week of being closed for renovations, the bakery was ready to reopen.

"The place looks amazing, by the way," he said. "Are you excited about reopening tomorrow?"

"Over the moon." She propped her hands on her hips. "Do you think the renovations work? It's not too much?"

The walls were mounted with framed pictures of Cedar River from past to present. Winnie had decorated the shop with old-fashioned baking utensils and mixers, and she'd even set up the pastry case to have a whole new look, all styled to pay homage to the town's rich history. He admired his wife's commitment to the project and was so proud that she'd realized her dream.

"It's perfect," he replied and moved toward her. "Like you."

She laughed and pressed against him. "Are you drunk?"

Grant grasped her chin gently. "Not a chance. Remember the trouble I got into the last time we had too much champagne?"

"But then we wouldn't have all this," she said, waving a hand between them and gesturing to their sleeping child.

"Oh, I don't know," Grant said and brought her closer. "I'd like to think we would have ended up here eventually."

She met his gaze. "Oh, no, I know that mushy look."

He smiled warmly, his heart rolling over. "Better get used to it, Mrs. Culhane."

"I am," she assured him. "I love that you're so sentimental these days."

Grant chuckled, because most days that's exactly how he felt. "Do you know what I love?" he asked, holding her close, kissing the soft spot below her ear. "You. Rorie. Our life together."

"No regrets?" she asked.

"Not one," he replied and felt the truth of his words seep through him. Some days, he couldn't believe he'd gotten so lucky. Being a husband and father had profoundly changed him. Loving Winnie made everything so right in his world and had also given him the courage to truly let go of his resentment toward Billie-Jack. "One day I'm gonna thank that marine for standing you up at the altar."

She smiled against his mouth, kissing him softly. "Me, too."

"I love you, Winnie."

Her lips curved. "Ditto."

And that, he thought as he kissed her, was all he needed to know.

* * * * *

Don't miss Joss's story,
the next installment of Helen Lacey's miniseries
The Culhanes of Cedar River
on sale September 2021
wherever Harlequin books and ebooks are sold.

COMING NEXT MONTH FROM

⒣ HARLEQUIN
SPECIAL EDITION

#2851 FOR HIS DAUGHTER'S SAKE
Montana Mavericks: The Real Cowboys of Bronco Heights
by Stella Bagwell

Sweet Callie Sheldrick disarms single dad Tyler Abernathy in ways he can't explain, but the widowed rancher is in no position for courting, and he won't ask Callie to take on another woman's child. The kindest thing he can do is to walk away. Yet doing the "right thing" might end up breaking all three of their hearts...

#2852 THE HORSE TRAINER'S SECRET
Return to the Double C • by Allison Leigh

When Megan Forrester finds herself pregnant, she resolves to raise the baby herself. But when Nick Ventura becomes the architect on a ramshackle Wyoming ranch Megan's helping friends turn into a home, that resolve soon weakens. After all, Nick's the total package—gorgeous, capable and persistent. Not to mention the father of her child! If only she could tell him...

#2853 THE CHEF'S SURPRISE BABY
Match Made in Haven • by Brenda Harlen

A family emergency whisks Erin Napper away before chef Kyle Landry can figure out if they've stirred up more than a one-night stand. Almost a year later, Erin confesses her secret to Kyle: their baby! But the marriage of convenience he proposes? Out of the question. Because settling for a loveless relationship would be like forgetting the most important ingredient of all.

#2854 THEIR TEXAS TRIPLETS
Lockharts Lost & Found • by Cathy Gillen Thacker

Cooper Maitland's nieces were left at the ranch for him, but this cowboy isn't equipped to take on three infants on his own. Jillian Lockhart owes Coop, so she'll help him look after the triplets for now—but recklessly falling in love would be repeating past mistakes. As they care for the girls together, can their guarded hearts open enough to become a family?

#2855 THEIR RANCHER PROTECTOR
Texas Cowboys & K-9s • by Sasha Summers

Skylar Davis is grateful to have her late husband's dog. But the struggling widow can barely keep her three daughters fed, much less a hungry canine. Kyle Mitchell was her husband's best friend and he can't stop himself from rescuing them. But will his exposed secrets ruin any chance they have at building a family?

#2856 ACCIDENTAL HOMECOMING
The Stirling Ranch • by Sabrina York

Danny Diem's life is upended when he inherits a small-town ranch. But learning he has a daughter in need of lifesaving surgery is his biggest shock yet. He'd never gotten over his ex Lizzie Michaels. But her loving strength for their little girl makes him wonder if he's ready to embrace the role he's always run from: *father*.

**YOU CAN FIND MORE INFORMATION ON UPCOMING HARLEQUIN TITLES,
FREE EXCERPTS AND MORE AT HARLEQUIN.COM.**

HSECNM0721

"Even the strongest people need a break now and then. It's
not a sign of being weak—it's part of being human," he
murmured against her temple. "As far as I'm concerned,
you're a badass."

She shook her head but didn't say anything.

"Look at your girls," he insisted. "You put those smiles
on their faces. You found a way to keep them entertained
and positive and with enough imagination to turn that
leaning wooden shack into a playhouse—"

"Hey," she interrupted, peering up at him with red-
rimmed eyes.

"I was teasing." He smiled. "You're missing the point
here."

"Oh?" She didn't seem fazed by the fact that she was still holding on to him—or that there was barely any space between them.

But he was. And it had him reeling. The moment her gaze met his, the tightness and pressure in his chest gave way. And having Skylar in his arms, soft and warm and all woman, was something he hadn't prepared himself for.

Focus. Not on the unnerving reaction Skylar was causing, but on being here for Skylar and the girls. *Focus on honoring Chad's last request.* Chad—who'd expected him to take care of the family he'd left behind, not get blindsided and want more than he should. How could he not? Skylar was a strong, beautiful woman who had his heart thumping in a way he didn't recognize.

"Thank you, again." Her gaze swept over his face before she rose on tiptoe and kissed his cheek. "You're a good man, Kyle Mitchell."

Don't miss
Their Rancher Protector *by Sasha Summers,*
available August 2021 wherever
Harlequin Special Edition books and ebooks are sold.

Harlequin.com

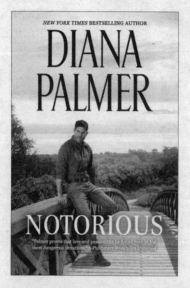

Love Harlequin romance?

DISCOVER.

Be the first to find out about promotions, news and exclusive content!

Facebook.com/HarlequinBooks

Twitter.com/HarlequinBooks

Instagram.com/HarlequinBooks

Pinterest.com/HarlequinBooks

ReaderService.com

EXPLORE.

Sign up for the Harlequin e-newsletter and download a free book from any series at
TryHarlequin.com

CONNECT.

Join our Harlequin community to share your thoughts and connect with other romance readers!
Facebook.com/groups/HarlequinConnection